Ashley Franz Holzmann

The Laws of Nature

A Collection of Short Stories of Horror, Anxiety, Tragedy and Loss

Book design and cover by Ashley Franz Holzmann

Edited by Tony Formica

Front cover font is Credit Valley, provided by Larabie Fonts

Printed in the United States of America

First Printing, 2014

ISBN 978-0692339633

As For Class
240 Captain's Harbor
Sanford, NC 27332

www.asforclass.com

To my wife

The Laws of Nature

When caught by a trap, a fox would rather gnaw off its own leg to escape than stay captured.

If you lock enough dogs in a room for long enough, they'll eat each other.

If a human artery is severed, exsanguination can take place within one minute.

I used to be a triplet.

Table of Contents

Introduction from the Editor	1
The Stump	5
Plastic Glasses	17
Putting Down Your Love	23
Crying Numbers	25
Checkpoint Charlie	43
Jolene Jolene Jolene Jolene	53
Hush	59
Soul Sucker	67
Good Time Charlie	71
See Me. Let Go.	77
Lady Macbeth	83
He Only Had Sex With Strangers	93
Laughing at Lunch	105
Maslow's Hierarchy of Needs	109
In My Father's House	115
Glass Houses	121

White Heads 127

Orpheus's Lot 137

Cold Static 145

Letter From The Author 151

Special Thanks 155

About The Author 157

Introduction From The Editor

What is horror? What distinguishes both the genre and the emotional experience from mere suspense? And what is it about horror that not only attracts the interest of readers and viewers, but somehow manages to entice them to again and again seek out that spine-tingling, hair-raising thrill ride of fear and exhilaration?

I first met Ashley Holzmann in the summer of 2005, when he and I were both two bright-eyed, comically enthusiastic freshmen entering West Point. Neither of us really had a clue as to what sort of journey we were both about to embark upon. Fate would eventually see to it that Ashley and I not only spent our formative first summer at the Academy together in the same small group, but also that we would go on to be in the same company and even be roommates for a semester. I spent many a night in the barracks over the ensuing years editing then-Cadet Holzmann's writing assignments; five years after graduation, I get the unique privilege of seeing Ashley truly come into his own with the debut of his first published anthology.

As I learned early on in my friendship with him, and as readers will shortly discover, Ashley has an ability to pierce through the facades, pretenses, and deeply held but poorly considered convictions of people to get to the heart of the impulses and needs that drive them. It is simultaneously one of the most refreshing and most unsettling attributes that he possesses—from our earliest days as plebes on the Hudson right through the present, Ashley has always been that rare individual who is able to leverage his emotional intelligence to make profound insights about people and organizations that elude those of us more shackled to reason and convention.

But readers beware: this West Point-educated, engineering-trained, trajectory-calculating former field artillery officer will also leverage data and statistics to substantiate what his intuition tells him. Ashley would spend his time at the Academy majoring in sociology, making him naturally predisposed to merge empirical discipline with the humanities to explain and predict human nature on a societal scale. Although, if one takes only a cursory glance at Ashley's life, one has to quickly concede that Ashley didn't require much formal schooling on social organization, disorder, or patterns—his life before the Academy already spanned four continents, seven countries, and countless interactions with distinct cultures, and his service in the Army has only deepened that rich reservoir of experience that is so clearly present in his writing.

What comes from Ashley's pen as a result of all of his background, training, and natural talents is a description of people for what they are, stripped of the petty little deceits they tell themselves and try to project onto others. Ashley's writing overflows with monologues many of us can relate to; emotional shades that we've likely dabbled in but never voiced because we tell ourselves we're better than that; and situations that disturb us, not because they are beyond belief, but because we only too well understand the tragic flaws that bring them about.

Which brings us back to the question I posed at the beginning of this introduction. What is horror? Certainly, in its modern conception it entails gore and violence. But I think that before that, and certainly after it, horror speaks to the latent fear inside each of us that we are both frail—physically and emotionally—and flawed entities, so often trying to rise above the vulnerabilities of our existence, and, more often than we would care to admit, failing at it. It is distinguished from suspense in its completeness: whereas suspense is defined as existing before an event, and is immediately followed by some form of catharsis, horror does not leave us so emotionally relieved and cleansed. Instead, horror progressively builds up its narrative and energy; it may reach a climax, or it might not, but very rarely is there ever resolution of such a degree that readers can confidently say: "It's over." Rather, horror leaves its audience with only the awful, disquieting possibility of recurrence.

And as for the audience that keeps coming back for more? That I leave to your own judgement—but I'll wager, somewhere behind the rush of excitement and the tantalizing enjoyment of the unknown lies a love for being made to feel just a little less secure in your conception of the world. That is the true lure in the stories that Ashley consolidated here, and I am confident that it is what will keep you reading through to the anthology's last disquieting possibility of recurrence.

Tony Formica
Leesville, Louisiana
October, 2014

The Stump

I never ran past the stump. Never. The stump had been there for years, at the edge of where I turned around on my runs, right at that point where I knew I would have a hard time getting back without walking.

Except for that day. Last spring, around noon on a Saturday. Gentle breeze, high 70s. The sun dipping behind the clouds every few minutes. Perfect weather.

Something about the daylight had always made me feel insecure. It was the night we were always supposed to be wary of, with its shadows and the silence. When the bugs would stop making noises—that's when you were supposed to worry. That's when the hairs were supposed to rise. When everything felt wrong. Not during the day, though. Not when everything was supposed to be safe.

That was never how I worked, though. I was always wary of the day growing up. My nightmares were during nap times, during the day when everyone else thought the world was safe.

I grew up as a cautious type of kid. I was afraid of a lot of things. Being alone used to terrify me. I slept in my parents' bed until I was four or five, and even after that I felt uneasy sleeping alone. Most kids feel safe if they bundle up enough in their blankets, but that never worked for me. I always felt as if I were lying on an island surrounded by evil, and nothing I could do could protect me from it.

Back in high school, running was easier. I could eat what I

wanted, and run whenever I felt like it. My run time was never really affected by my life choices. I was a quick kid, too. I was running low five-minute miles. One time I even ran a 4:50. Not really competition speeds for college, but pretty good for a kid who just enjoyed going to city runs on the weekends.

I used to imagine myself as a gazelle, running from a cheetah or some other large cat. The cats win sometimes, but the gazelle has form over power, grace over strength. When chased, the gazelle will take every step with the intent to survive. That need to live always spoke to me.

That was the past. As the years strode by, running six-minute miles began to hurt. I became more of a seven-minute mile type. Which was fine; I wasn't racing anymore.

For me, running had always been a form of meditation. About a mile or so into a run everything would loosen up and it'd become easier to stride out. Mentally, I'd reach a point where the intense focus I needed to maintain pace simply melted away and I became more of a spectator than a participant in the run. I would experience myself as just a part of the trail.

On that Saturday, everything felt right. Everything was more than fine. It was the perfect day. I was approaching the stump and I felt amazing. The best I had felt on a run in years.

Years.

I approached the stump and I hurdled over it like a track star. I heard a scratching sound, even though it felt like a clean jump and I didn't feel like I scraped anything. I was so in the zone that I didn't turn around. Birds and other animals in the woods were common on my runs. I ended up running another mile into the forest. I had never been that deep in. I was probably around five miles from my house when I saw a bit of smoke in the distance. I knew that there were other trails in the woods, but the trail I used was the nice one. The trail that the sun could touch almost all day.

I looked down. My trail had quickly devolved. It wasn't as nice as it was before the stump.

I saw the smoke get closer. Then I saw a shape.

It was a cottage. The smoke was coming from a random cottage deep in the woods, a building so run-down the squirrels likely avoided it. Something about the way the house sat on its foundation made it seem to be twisted and, in a way, abnormal. The windows were uncharacteristically high, beginning almost at chest level. I started to jog in place, considering whether or not to keep moving forward or to turn back. The curtains in the window had some sort of floral pattern. I didn't want to trespass. I never knew who the woods really belonged to out here.

Suddenly, the curtain was thrown back and a figure was looking at me from behind the window. Eyes wide, barely peering over the base of the windowsill.

I turned and I ran toward home.

It seemed so far. It took me a very long time to make it back to the woods I was familiar with. I just kept running. Pumping my arms and moving my legs. Breathing. Strong inhale. Strong exhale. Strong inhale. Strong exhale. Focus. Equal breathing. Equal breathing.

That's when I saw the stump. Except it didn't look the same, different from how I was used to seeing it. Granted, I had never approached the stump from that side before. But I knew. I knew that there was something wrong. My chest tensed up just a little bit more. I slowed down to give some rest to my hips.

There was some sort of lump on the tree stump that I had never seen. Some type of cancer.

The closer I got, the less the lump looked like a part of the tree. It looked like some kind of matted hair, clumped and moist. I had slowed down to almost a walk. I was just a few strides away from the stump when the moist lump opened its eyes.

It was some type of animal, covered in a dark brown fur that almost camouflaged it against the stump's bark. It was only after the eyes opened that I realized both of the animal's long arms were draped over my side of the stump, the head concealed behind the opposite side. All I could see were the eyes peeking over, like the animal was hiding from me.

"Hiiiiiiii, Alllllexander. Alexander the stranger. The runner, the Lone Ranger. Don't look surprissssssed. You don't remember me? We used to be so close. You slept on top of the bed, and I slept bellllllow," it said.

Its way of speaking seemed to trail off on certain words in a weird distracted tone. I looked at the arms of the animal, covered in hair, powerful looking. I couldn't bring myself to speak, at first. I hesitated. "Are you the devil?"

"Aw, Alexxxx, the devil is just a story. I'm very real. I'm you. I'm not you. I'm something different. Something blue. Something betterrrrrrrr," it said. The animal started to tap the stump's bark with all of its fingers.

"I need to go. I want to go home," I said. I was looking at the hands of the animal, at the claws. It was tapping its fingers against the bark. I noticed my breathing wasn't rapid. I wasn't out of breath at all from the run. Instead, I was barely breathing at all. Like I kept forgetting to take another breath every few seconds. I turned my head to look back at the cottage quickly to see if anything was coming from that direction. Nothing was there. I quickly turned my head back to keep my eyes on the creature behind the stump.

"Ohhh, nowwww, Alex. Don't you worry about Mother. You'll never get to meet her, Allllllexxxx. That's what I'm here for. You shouldn't have looked. Didn't you learn to never peek under the bed, Allleexxx? Triple X. Not the sex. Not the sex. You aren't going where you want to. This isn't the trail home. The trail of tears. The trail of fears. We're going to do something else," it said. Up until that point the eyes had been wandering, contemplating what the next words would be. The animal seemed to enjoy the rhymes. Every rhyme would strike some sort of emotional chord with my childhood. The shows I watched, the things I would say growing up.

Then the animal's eyes locked right into mine. "The things I'm going to do to you, Alex. Oh, you haven't lived until you've, ahhhhhhh, the things I will do to your innards. The belly. Inside. I don't want to ruin the surprise, but, ohhhh. The things we are going. To. Do." I heard it clack its teeth together a few times.

I swallowed and reminded myself to breathe. I made myself say something. "Please. Don't," was all that came out.

I couldn't see its mouth, but I could imagine its smile. It was in the eyes. Everything about the animal was inhuman, except for the eyes. Baby blues. They could have been my eyes. The eyes squinted a little in an expression dripping with intent. "Are you going to pee yourself? Are you going to pisssssss? Little Alex pissed the bed. Pissed the bed and slept in the shed. You can't hide from me, Alex. You can't run away. This is our moment, together. Are you going to pee pee? Cry to Mother. I used to lick it up, every time I would lick it all up. I would suck that bed dry after a good soiling. What it must taste like after all these years. I've waited, Alex. I've waited to taste it from the source. Pure. Unfiltered. I've followed you for a very long time. Go ahead and do it for me, Alex. I just want to smell it," the animal said.

I heard it lick its lips and start clicking its teeth. I could hear them like pieces of metal clacking together. And then the animal slowly raised its head above the stump. There was no smile. Just a wide mouth of teeth. Row upon row into the blackness of its throat. As if the teeth would never end once something strayed past the animal's hairy lips. "No," was all I could say.

"No? Oh, Alex. We know no won't go. No. I'm going to step over this stump and you are going to let me do it. All the dreams are about to happen. Let me suck on it. Your hand, your foot, your leg, your flesh. Just a nibble. Just the tipssssss." The animal began to laugh. Seeing the teeth, hearing the laughter, the depth of the animal's scratchy voice. Like coals on a fire.

My bladder let out everything.

The moment that happened, the animal stopped laughing and threw its head back in the air to take in the smell. I could see its nostrils expand to surprising size. Maybe fear drove me, because once I realized the animal was going to keep its head back a moment, I shot into the edge of the woods to the right. Fight or flight.

That day was my best run in so long that I had to chance it. I had to try to escape. To run for my life. Miles. I still had miles until I would make it back home. And I wasn't on any trail; I was just running through the middle of the woods, hitting the dead pine needles with my feet. Needles that were never cleared by anyone. You could have buried anything in those woods. If someone disappeared out there, that would have been it.

The animal realized a few seconds after I broke the tree line that I wasn't going to wait. I didn't hear it talk, but I did hear it start moving behind me. The movement was what kept me sprinting, kept me pushing myself. I heard the legs of the creature and the trees. The animal was so strong that every few breaths I was taking I would hear a tree get splintered, or another tree fall down. And it was gaining on me.

Another tree fell. I could hear the animal breathing. "Allllllexxxxxx," it said. "Alex," I couldn't turn around. I didn't want to. If it weren't for the lack of a trail, I would have closed my eyes, hidden deep inside myself and hoped to wake up alive. The breathing was so close, almost right next to my ears. I didn't want to see. I didn't want to see the moment happen. I wanted to try to fight until the very end.

And that's when I found another trail.

Out of nowhere. It was going in the same direction as the main trail I had always ran down. I didn't think of anything besides getting home and escaping. I opened up my stride and I did my best to breathe correctly. Pump my arms, perfect form, perfect form. Not slamming my feet, not arching my back too much, staying forward, letting my core be involved. It was the most important run of my life.

I was the gazelle. Puff out.

I had to be. Gasp in.

I needed to be perfect. Puff out.

I needed to live. Gasp in.

I knew I had a chance if I could sustain the pace, maintain, and not look back. Even on the trail, I could still hear the animal crashing through the woods behind me, as if the trail wasn't wide enough. I didn't want to think about how massive it was, how easily the animal was going to tear me apart, how my skin was going to feel sliding off my bones.

I tried to keep my mind on the run. On the breathing. On staying light. Falling on each step to save energy. Long strides. I could make it if I kept form. Kept the breathing, ignored the pain in my shins, in my thighs. I had been past muscle failure when I ran past the stump; I wasn't sure how I was running as well as I was then but I knew I wanted to live. Knew that if I kept that in my mind, I could do it.

I was so close. I saw the edge of the woods, and there was maybe a quarter of a mile before I was out. I was there. I was going to make it. The animal kept running after me. It must have had many legs, given how it was smashing through the bushes and tearing apart the trees.

Ten feet away from the wood line, I took a step but my foot didn't land right. The animal had caught me by grabbing a hold of my ankle. I was pulled to the ground and my head hit something while I was being flipped upside down. The animal raised me up to its face. "Alex, I love games. I told you that you couldn't run. Was that tortuuuurrrreee for you? I let you get this far."

The animal's tongue came out of its mouth. Long and grotesque, the tongue slipped down my shorts to taste the urine. It was a violating sensation. Sandpaper. If I hadn't already done so, I would have urinated myself, again. "Salty," the animal chuckled.

I was shaking. There's a certain type of anticipation that the body experiences when the mind knows everything is about to end. I could feel it in the back of my neck. A kind of tingle. Instead of forgetting to breathe, I couldn't get enough air. My lungs were a vacuum.

I was upside down, but raised high enough to be eye level with the animal. The creature was something old and eternal: the hair matted in odd places, patches of scales, sharp joints of a being that should have died when the planet was young. My heart ached. To be so close to home and to be gazing upon true evil. The monster. The devil. To see the matted hair and the black line over the blue eyes. "Oh, Alex, sweety. No tears? Now now, do stop screaming. No one can hear you in this terrible dream," the animal said. The smell was too complicated for human noses to understand; it was disgusting and as hot as a furnace.

My skin felt tighter after each breath from the creature.

And the animal was right, I was screaming. I didn't even realize it, my mind was in so many places. I couldn't think of anything to do. I was trapped. Caught. "Please," was the only word I managed to get out.

"Don't mind if I do, boy." What happened next was fast. I was instantly flipped right-side up and I watched as the animal opened its mouth wide. All those teeth seemed to be infinite. An impossibly deep throat. A part of my mind thought I was looking into Hell itself.

There was no fire, just the heat of it. There were only teeth.

The animal's tongue slid out of the mouth and wrapped around my leg and drifted up. I tried to struggle away, but there was nowhere to go in that amount of time. I saw my leg slowly being pulled into the mouth. The end. I closed my eyes.

My skin slid off of the bone like the icicle on a popsicle stick. I felt the tug, the pressure, and then heard a pop and a feeling of release. At first, I couldn't tell if the fire that shot up my leg was the heat from the animal's mouth or the pain. It was searing. I couldn't help but look. See what had happened. I was bleeding everywhere. So much blood drenched the animal's face. I realized why the animal's fur was all matted. Clotted. It had its eyes closed, enjoying the blood spraying all over its face. Half of my leg was gone, disappeared in the animal's mouth. The pain was everywhere, and I was surprised that I had not immediately gone into shock. I knew that I needed to keep my head together. I needed to concentrate. Then I heard the crunching. The animal started to chew.

It was eating my leg.

It dropped me to the ground. It seemed to be caught up in the sensation. Like it hadn't eaten in years. I didn't care. I needed to escape, I needed to get home. Home. I was almost in my backyard. I was ten feet away. There was so much blood, I knew I had only a few minutes. Maybe less. I needed to get to my back yard, I needed to crawl. I rolled over to my stomach and I moved every remaining limb as fast as I could. "No. Ugh, uk! Stuck! Stop!" the animal choked out in surprise. The animal's mouth was full. I had the notion that it didn't want to stop chewing. It paused, as if to decide whether it should just enjoy what it had, or to catch me. Maybe it paused intentionally. By the time the animal made the decision to lunge at me, I had rolled the rest of the way into my backyard. I had done it. I made it back. I rolled to my back. I knew I needed to stop the bleeding. Seconds mattered. I ripped off all of my clothes and tore them to tie a tourniquet. I pulled the knots tight and covered the stump that remained of my leg.

My heart was still beating.

I needed to hydrate.

I needed to.

I needed to get to a doctor.

I needed.

I needed.

I passed out.

I woke up. I couldn't tell how long I'd been out. I looked over. Maybe it had all just been a dream. A nightmare, and I had become dehydrated on my run. It was a relieving feeling, but after a moment the clouds in my head started to clear. It wasn't a dream. At the edge of the woods, it was there. Peeking behind a tree, and somehow hiding the true size of itself. The animal.

It was dangling a shredded running shoe in one of its hands. My running shoe. I heard a slow crunching sound. A steady chewing. The animal was still chewing on my bones. It began to speak again, except its voice had changed to the voice of my mother, "Alex. Allllleeeexxx, wake up, sweatheart. It's time to go outside and play. Go off and play in the woods. Don't you want to come back, honey? Do come back. Maybe tomorrow, yes? Get your five miles in. Get your ten miles in? I'll see you then, dear. I will see you then." I never could figure out what made the animal stop, how it wasn't able to move past the wood line, or even how I knew I would be safe if I made it back to my yard. Was it really under my bed as a child? The cottage. Mother. I didn't understand.

I crawled back to my house. The bleeding had slowed, but the bandages were soaked through with my blood. I was really lightheaded. I thought I was going to pass out again when I had to push the sliding glass door open.

I managed to make a phone call before passing out again.

The doctors didn't know what to think. I told them it was a gator that got me. No one would have believed anything else. No one questioned me further with that information, either. People rarely show up at an ER with a leg bitten off. No doctor where I live would have the experience to really question my story, anyway.

I have never gone back in the woods. Never even thought about it. I never could go back. Sometimes, if I wake up before the sun rises, I'll be drinking my coffee and right when the sun hits the tree line, I'll see it. The animal, peeking out from behind a trunk. Never the same tree. What is left of my leg will ache, and I'll feel the sensation of being lowered into the animal's mouth, again. The tip of my leg will feel that fire. The tip of *my* stump.

Once the twilight of morning is past, the animal will duck from whatever it's hiding behind and disappear. It never speaks. It never does anything but look at me. I never see the animal's teeth, but I don't ever have to.

Plastic Glasses

I was twelve years old when I wrote my first suicide note. Growing up, I would hear the same line constantly: "Our family had a history of mental illness and depression, and that's why this or that happened."

That speech was the number one excuse for just about everything my mother did. If we lived in a honeycomb of lies and self-deception, then my mother was the queen bee of excuses. And while it bugged me, I always forgave her because, you know, she was my mother. Back then, I just figured she was always going through rough stuff.

She was manic. She'd be the happiest being on the planet one day, making me breakfast and packing a lunch; she'd clean the house up and be at my soccer game that night. She relished cheering me on. I said "clean," but that wasn't right. Our house was always a mess. "Clean" just meant that you could walk into all of the rooms except the garage—that place was a wasteland. We'd go home and build puzzles and chat about nonsense. We'd have these totally perfect days where the universe just clicked and life was great because it was her and me knocking it out of the park.

But then she'd have the bad days and life would suck our house dry. My mom's room would become this utter neutral zone where everything happy would go to die, and she'd just blare the TV on the worst channels. She'd soak in reality television and she'd talk about how horrible those people were for living their lives that way. Mom would stay up way too late and not wake up on time to make me breakfast, and I'd pack my own lunches. I'd walk home from school when she'd forget to pick me up. It wasn't so bad; the upside was that the long walks kept me in shape for soccer.

I'd get home and wake her up. We'd eat a TV dinner, ramen, or pizza on our plastic plates, with our plastic silverware, while we sat in our plastic chairs. We would look at the sink, filled with plastic. Sometimes we'd joke about how we would do the dishes that upcoming weekend, but we never would.

In a lot of ways, I was like my mother. Even back then, I could see that. I knew what I was becoming, and I knew it was due largely to her influence. It didn't matter what friends I picked, it didn't matter what books I'd sink myself into, or how often I'd try to do the self-improvement thing: my mother would always be there to either build me up or break me down to her level. If she was going through something dark, the world was going along for the ride.

I lost a lot of friends because of her. I mean, not directly, but indirectly. I'd be talking to a new friend and we'd get super close, and then I just wouldn't be as chipper one day, or maybe mom was going through a rough patch and I'd just kind of burn the bridge. I'd say something petty or cruel, and then I'd be back the next day acting like nothing happened. I basically built a negative persona. I was the psycho chubby chick who wore too much black, or tried too hard, or couldn't find a boy or thought about cutting. I was just trying to make up for being so crappy. Being a kid sucks. And girls can be mean.

Sometimes I would think about what life would have been like if mom had taken her meds all the time. When she was on them, she wouldn't have the low points, but she also wouldn't ever get those high moments. The moments where she and I were a real family. When she was on the meds, though, we never had those times where we'd click. We'd just sit around the table or the TV and kind of chill out. Which wasn't bad, except that she was so boring. I knew she wasn't happy living like that. So when she wouldn't take the meds, I never really blamed her. I mean, I partly did, like you blame a dog for shitting in the house. It's irritating, but also somewhat expected. Looking back, I can see why she would say "screw it."

Mom was cool about a lot of things. She let me pretend I had boyfriends and she would never call me out on it when I talked about how popular I was. Maybe she even really believed me. She'd be pretty chill about letting me watch whatever I wanted to on TV. And she never checked my homework or any of that sort of tiger mom stuff.

I guess if I had to boil everything down between her and me, I'd have to say my feelings are pretty complicated. I became the person I am because of the love she showed me. But I also turned out the way I did because of the stuff she put me through. Like, who gives their little girl cigarettes? I still can't bring myself to quit. And I never recovered from any of the advice she would give me about how to deal with bullies. Everything I would try would just make it worse and worse. It was so overwhelming, and the one person I needed to stand up for me would just shrug that stuff off and tell me life sucked. That wasn't really what I needed to hear. Where were those talks about making friends, or how to be the cool kid, or how to not screw up friendships? I wanted the adult and I was being raised by the child.

Anyways.

Yeah.

I came home one day. And the entire house was clean. The floors, the kitchen, the living room. For a moment, I thought that my mother had abandoned me. But then it clicked when I saw what she had left out.

My mother had left out a paper bag packed with a lunch dated for the next day, and a half completed puzzle on our dining room table. The plastic in the sink had all been washed and put away. She didn't need to leave a note: I knew what it all meant.

I ran throughout the entire house. Room to room. Ever since Dad had left, we had the whole place packed full of useless stuff, but with it all gone I had no idea where to look for her. The last place I thought to look was the garage. When I threw open the door, there she was, hanging from the ceiling, kicking and thrashing. At first it wasn't happening—that sort of thing couldn't really happen. But in an instant the adrenaline and reality of the moment pushed me into the room and toward my mother. She was still alive. She was scratching at the rope and I knew I could save her if I could just lift her high enough.

But I was twelve.

And I just… couldn't. I stood there, holding my mother up for a long time. Trying to hold her up high enough to keep the rope slack, but I wasn't strong enough. The rope wasn't slack. The kicking had stopped probably hours before I finally let myself let go of her. In the end, she had laid a hand on top of my head. Like everything was totally alright.

My legs were so tired from trying to lift her that I had to sit down. I sat there for a long time.

Her face had been scratched up from when she tried to grab the rope. Her beautiful face.

All of my life, I had been told that depression and mental illness ran in my family. While I was growing up, that never used to bother me. So what, right? But, now, it keeps me up at night. Knowing that the only person I loved in my life was capable of something so low. She must have been in a pretty dark place.

And, well, I didn't want her to leave without saying everything she needed to say. I didn't want to just call the cops and spill the story. I didn't even know how to begin a phone conversation like that. I was twelve. She needed closure. I needed closure. So I found some paper and wrote my mother's suicide note the best way I could. I didn't want the cops to think she was totally insane, because sometimes I felt the way she must have. It ran in the family. Sometimes, when I'm feeling really low, I reread the note. A note written on the cleanest table I had ever seen in my life. The smell of pine not helping with the tears. I wrote that note in a house that wasn't mine. My home was a home of cluttered genius, a home of TV dinners and soda and dust mites and pizza boxes. Maybe it was the fakest moment of my life. Maybe it was the most real moment I had ever experienced. My final effort to appease my mother through an act of self-delusion.

The note written by the sunshine version of my mother, as I remember the woman she could be. The potential she had to live a beautiful life was amazing. I'll always love her for that, but she didn't finish building the puzzle.

Putting Down Your Love

The hardest moment of my life was today, when I had to put down my sweet Rex.

You raise them and wean them from their mothers so you can become their mother. Their new family. Their real family. That's all you really want.

You walk them and feed them and you follow the rules. You fast them once a week to keep their digestive systems in shape.

Clip their toenails. Even when they don't want it.

Housetrain them.

Sleep with them.

Pet them.

You love them. Because you saved them from whatever awful life they could have had. Without protection, without your special brand of love, they would have never made it. You were their hero. The one they couldn't wait to see every day.

Sometimes you had to discipline them, but it wasn't because you enjoyed that. Chaining them up out back, maybe fasting them an extra day. It's important to be able to see their ribs and such. The look in their eyes after they finally learn is how you know it's worth it. It's not about the power or the control. It's just about the love. You want them to love you and you want them to follow the rules.

But, having to say goodbye.

If they bite, you're supposed to put them down. We can't have biting. We live out deep in the country, and we don't have anyone else to do those sorts of things. We have to do it ourselves. Looking into those eyes, knowing they don't quite understand—that doesn't come easy.

Today, in that moment, I could barely keep it all together. I bawled while I stood there, about ready for the end.

"I love you, Rex," I said.

"I love you too, Mama."

And then I pulled the trigger.

Crying Numbers

The first week.

It's all in the numbers. That's how you understand anything of real value in this world.

At this point, we don't need the baby monitor anymore. But even after all this time, I still need the static to fall asleep. It was a while ago when the baby started sleeping through the night, and I needed it through that transition. The monitor has one of those screens, too, that turns on if there is movement in the room. It really doesn't turn on anymore. But sometimes I'll wake up in the middle of the night and press the *on* button. Just to look.

Just to remind myself.

A healthy male in his prime will produce anywhere from around thirty million to an excess of one billion sperm during an ejaculation. Of that group, only so many make it to the fallopian tubes—fewer than twenty sperm ever reach the egg. Sometimes none make it.

I had met my wife in high school, but we didn't date until after college. She went her way, I went mine, and for some reason both of us backwoods kids ended up in Panama City at the same beach during spring break. It was the kind of scenario we both completely hid from our parents, but that was the beginning. The first kiss escalated into a lot of other firsts that we just sort of blew right through that week. We had come so far since then. Getting married, the honeymoon in Florida. We decided to put our careers on hold and spend a few years together. It was a good call. But that was also before we started doing the math for everything. Realizing that we'd be in our fifties once the kids left the house. And that was if we had the first kid nine months after we started trying.

When it comes to trying to get pregnant, ovulation is at the center of everything. Ovulation is only a little window. Certain religions even track cycles so they can have unprotected sex around the ovulation cycle to prevent pregnancy. Even if a couple has unprotected sex and is trying to conceive, the odds are only stacked so much in their favor. A couple trying to get pregnant can still find themselves without child after a year. Something like 10-15% will take longer than a year to get pregnant.

You know, the real irony of having children with my wife was that we were actually both in the same health class together. Mr. Schuller was this old conservative values man from the middle of the century. He didn't teach us much, but he did manage to tell us interesting anecdotal tales that had nothing to do with sex or reproduction. He never did tell us the odds of anything. None of the real numbers.

Like the odds for miscarriages. Most people don't ever look these up, so they don't realize that a spontaneous abortion can take place at any point during the first twenty weeks, but mostly just the first thirteen. And the numbers get smudged on this one, but the odds of a miscarriage are around one in five. Some experts believe the odds are three out of five. If it happens early enough, an uneducated mother-to-be will think it was just a late period.

When we finally decided to have children, it took us two years to get pregnant. And not just two years of trying to not try. We were actively trying. Two years of almost treating it like our part-time job. It took a bit of the fun out of it, actually. But we knew we both wanted it. We were more than ready for that next phase of our lives.

When it finally happened, we were so happy. My wife was the one who told me we had to wait a few weeks. She told me how common miscarriages were and that's what got me started on the numbers. On knowing the odds.

Most mothers don't know to wait. They take the pregnancy test and they let everyone know they got the pink little circle or the triangle or the double lines. Then the doctor visit takes place and the baby's gone. They never did the research to know how frequent it all is, how often things don't work out. And the reasons are countless. Sometimes the body just rejects the baby. Other times, the mother smoked or drank too much caffeine or some other drug. Or maybe the mother is over 45 years old, in which case their odds jump up to a fifty-fifty chance of keeping the baby to term. Sometimes, it just happens. No one's to blame and something just doesn't line up.

We also went through a few false alarms in those two years. We made it pretty far at one point. We were a week away from telling our friends and family when my wife had another period. It was a rough point in our life together. But we kept trying. We knew it would happen, eventually.

Once your child's born, there's a one in 1,500 chance that it will pass away from SIDS (Sudden Infant Death Syndrome). They just fall asleep one day and never wake up again. No one has completely figured out why. If the mother is seriously ill, the odds go up that the child will have difficulty. Any number of external factors limit the chances for the baby: smoking, drinking, eating wrong, drugs, even getting the flu. In America, the child mortality rate of children that don't make it past their fifth birthday is around five for every one thousand. In some countries, it's above a hundred for every thousand. America's current population is around 310 million.

When we finally were able to tell our friends and family, I was so happy. We were making it; when we found out it would be a boy, happiness grew into pride. We took classes; pride turned to paranoia. We bought padding for everything, stocked up on band-aids and medicines and bought enough diapers to last us a year.

All those odds.

All those numbers stacked against all of us. And it has even gotten better over the years. That our species has survived this long is always a wonder to me, when I sit down and consider it all.

I guess you could say I was a nervous father. During our pregnancy, every day felt like a miracle. The idea that life was being molded in there. That our bits of protoplasm were forming into something that we would later shape in other ways, and which would shape us, was the most amazing feeling I had ever experienced.

Through the screaming and the drugs and the sleepless nights, there he was. The more perfect version of ourselves. Still pure from his lack of experience with the world. Not yet touched by the harshness.

We did our best to be informed. It was pretty hard stepping up to the plate with that. Cynthia was too drugged up to say yes or no to things, so there I was, remembering the classes and remembering what to say *no* to. What to say *yes* to. They try to sell you anything in that moment. Most of the time they just want to get off shift early. You can't blame them too much, I guess. A job's a job. And I have no reason to be bitter about our experience at the hospital. But there were a few moments where I thought they were trying to get over on us. I just had to keep reminding myself about everything. You can learn a lot from history. I mean, up into the 1950s doctors were still telling women to smoke while they were pregnant and they took x-rays of the babies.

Rhythms are quickly established during the first few days. Sleep when the baby sleeps. Anyone who doesn't do that deserves to be tired. Babies are like cats with regards to the number of hours they sleep. Once the newborn wakes up, you just go through the motions. Change, feed, burp, rock. Sleep.

But, then, last night happened. I had the monitor on and I fell asleep to the static low hum with the volume set at 40%, just in case. At four o'clock in the morning, the baby started screaming hard. It was the loudest, most terrible scream I had ever heard him put forth. There's something inside you when you become a parent. Something inside that doesn't make those screams annoying. Instead, when it's your baby, you just feel the screams like blows to the gut. I would do anything to soothe my little guy. Anything to make him feel better.

I would do anything to hold him. To give him that comfort.

To hold him, again.

It was all in the numbers, somewhere. That's how it always was and how it always is. Anything of real value has to be measured. And life is the most valuable of all things.

He screamed for thirty minutes over the monitor. The motion sensor even came on, he was so active. My wife and I just laid there.

The baby had passed away two weeks ago.

SIDS.

—

The second week.

Mr. Schuller was the type of teacher that tried to tell stories to make points that never related to the lesson. He was always trying to teach clumsy ethical lessons during health class, pushing his opinions and way of life with the cavalier arrogance of a Bible-thumping illiterate. To be honest, most of us just let all that stuff flow in and out of our ears. But in hindsight, some of those stories were good for a young teenager to hear. They must have made some sort of imprint, I can still remember them.

Mr. Schuller once spoke for forty minutes about the future of wireless technology. How the future would be all about wireless this and wireless that. This was around a year or so before any of us had heard of WiFi. Dial-up modems were still the way to access the Internet, and we all had to wait a hot minute for the static and noise to run its course while we dialed in. Mr. Schuller told us how wireless was not a new thing. How an inventor named Tesla had done experiments with electricity that spanned miles and only consisted of wireless transmissions of energy. There was a whole strange point to the story, but that part has since been lost to me. All I remember is visualizing the light bulbs turning on at such a distance. It's the image I think of every time the baby monitor hums.

When that screen pops on from the motion in my son's room, I think of Tesla. I think of the wireless transmission to the baby monitor and I wonder how the energy is used.

Last night was the night I decided to stay awake. Four o'clock was always the time the motion began, when the movements in my son's room would turn the monitor's light on. When the noises would start.

Same exact time.

Every single night.

But last night, I decided I would change one of the variables. After three weeks, I needed to know. I was ready to start dealing with the loss and ready to start understanding what was happening. That's what I told myself, how I rationalized.

The night dragged on, but I was able to stay awake. There was a low level of adrenaline keeping me on the edge, like the feeling kids get when they know Christmas is in the morning, except devoid of the joyful anticipation. I was blindfolded on a rollercoaster, going up a hill, and I had no clue when I'd take the plunge or how steep it would be.

I thought of my son and the last months he was alive. How we used to play around. I had gotten him a small stuffed fox with deep orange fur and beady eyes. He loved the thing and would tackle it to cuddle against its plush fiery fur. For the life of me I couldn't find it anywhere after his death. It had just disappeared.

I stared at the clock on the night stand until it clicked over. Four o'clock. Right on schedule, my son started to cry. Last night was the first night I considered the numbers involved. Four was never a time that he would normally wake up. My son was always asleep until at least six. I tried to remember if he cried the night he passed away. If maybe he warned us and this was a way for us to finally get there in time. A way for us to do the right thing.

Parents sleep so little in those first months. It was entirely possible for us to sleep through him crying at four if he woke up several times throughout the night. I couldn't remember. But thinking about it made me feel guilty. I shook my head and sat up to look at the monitor. Three weeks of listening to my son cry and I never had the guts to pick up the monitor to look. I wasn't sure what I would see. I licked my lips to get the dryness out of my mouth. I reached to pick up the monitor and took a long breath. The room was so dark that looking at the screen was blinding for a few seconds. I had to let my eyes adjust, and when they did, I was gazing right into the crib. The sound of crying continued coming from the piece of plastic, wirelessly transmitting its way into my hands.

There was something there, something dark and blurry, but it wasn't my son. I couldn't tell what it was. It was almost like it was canceling out the pixels on the LCD screen. I had been waiting for so long to see him again, I never thought I would be staring at something that wasn't a child. At a crying black blob of nothing. Was I crying, too? Maybe. I was having a hard time rationalizing what was happening, having a hard time breathing. My hands were shaking. And a tingling feeling kept creeping up and down my spine.

I had my finger on the *power* button, just to check. I needed to turn off the monitor for a moment. To let go. To say goodbye to my son. Three weeks of listening to the hum and then the cries was enough for me. My son was gone, and I needed to be able to accept that. Then, the black blob shifted and turned. It had eyes that radiated light, and the eyes looked right into the camera. Right into me.

I turned off the monitor as quickly as I could and tried to make myself continue to breathe. My brain wanted me to hyperventilate; my body wanted to do nothing except retreat into itself. I didn't know what the blob was, or what it being there meant. I was trying to figure it out when I realized that the monitor was off, but the crying sounds of my son hadn't stopped. The cries were real, and still coming from the other room.

I was shaking from the tingling feeling in my spine. But I decided to look. I needed to see. I looked over to my wife. She was still asleep. She always was. A part of me didn't think she even ever heard the monitor. But the sound was clear and audibly coming from our son's room.

He was still crying.

I got out of bed and made my way to my son's room. The cries got louder as I got closer, as though they were being amplified. I reached the door. A part of me hoped to see my son again. To hold him. For everything to be a dream or some strange hallucination. He was still alive and well. SIDS never happened. What were the odds of that? I didn't know. For once, I didn't care. I forced myself to take a breath and I opened the door.

The second the door was open the sound of my son's cries escalated to an intensely high pitch. Whatever was in the crib shot up to a sitting position. The eyes glowed with fire and they turned to look right at me. My ears were burned with the sound. The creature's mouth was moving to the cries. It was the source of the sound. It had replaced my son. I couldn't understand what was happening.

My wife was the only reason I woke up this morning. She found me on the floor outside my son's room, the door to his room still closed. My clothes were gone and dried blood caked on the sides of my head, rivers of crusted red flowing from my ears. My body was covered in scratches. I asked my wife if she heard any of the noises from last night.

"What noises?" she asked.

—

The third week.

It's been a rough week. I haven't woken up in my own bed for a few days now. Sometimes I remember getting into bed. Sometimes I'm going about my day and I simply wake up and it's morning. The stress has started to force me away from my wife. Or maybe it's her distancing herself from me. We never talk about it, leaving me to assume that this is just her own way of coping. It's logical.

People react to things differently. Her reaction has always been to sleep. To roll over. To zone out. She would do that all the time back in high school. Health class would start to get boring and she would go to the bathroom, do her thing. For some reason, I find myself thinking a lot of those days. How I used to stare at her in class. Fantasize about her when I'd get home from school. How much of my life started in high school? Why would those days never leave me? What if we had just never had a son?

Every day I wake up, it's to the sound of myself screaming. Just like the sensation of urinating in your sleep, the dream revolves around the scream. A slow fade gradually brings the scream out of the dream and I realize I'm the one making the noise. Making the bed yellow. Bleeding on a carpet somewhere in the house. Some mornings I'm downstairs. Most mornings I'm at the door to my son's room. The door is always closed. The last few days it's been locked.

I've asked my wife about it, about the door, but she persists in giving me the silent treatment. I've been getting mostly stares instead of conversation. I feel like I'm back in high school, passing notes to try and communicate and having girls look at me like I'm a fool for asking them out.

My wife has even changed her clothes. Like she doesn't want to wear the things I bought her. Or maybe the clothes remind her of our son. That would be reasonable. Sometimes I notice. Sometimes it's like the clothes change in the middle of the day. Nothing extreme, just a color here, a hat there. It throws off the day just enough to be devoid of sense. Sometimes it takes me an hour to pinpoint it.

Sometimes she reminds me of Alice, another girl that I sat near in health class back in high school. Alice was something. She always wore white. My wife was Cynthia, though. Cyn. She is Cyn. We used to have fun. Back when we were dating. We would take turns DDing and we would just tear up a town. Sometimes we'd go out parking, even though we each had a place. And when it came to serious adult life, she was wonderful. Every time I got sick, she was there for me. Ice cream, back rubs, the works. It was enough for me to propose. I knew I wanted to spend forever with her. To be the one to dote on her when she'd get sick. The good old days. It wasn't that long ago, but it feels like it was a lifetime.

Sometimes, when my son was inconsolable, I would turn on the TV. I was always lucky and found the right channel with the same shows. The dumb coyote never did win out. Always had an anvil or a ton of bricks landing on him. He seemed to have all the money in the world for gadgets, but lived out his life as a poor man. Never understood the meaning there. I suppose it was something about what's right in front of a man—how that stuff should make him happy. Either way, my son ate up the vaudeville. Every time.

Tangents. I never seem to tell a story straight through.

Last night, I didn't leave the monitor on. At least, I didn't remember keeping it on. Maybe I did and I just lowered the volume. The nights have started to blur. It's been a few weeks, now. It didn't matter, either way: the cries started at the same time, and I heard them all the same.

For me, the most haunting part of this experience has been that I was the worried parent. I was the one who couldn't sleep through him crying. I just couldn't take it. I was paranoid about everything. I'd wake up every hour or two and walk into my son's room and just check up on him. Check the thermostat to ensure it wasn't too warm or too cold. Leave the nightlight in the hallway on. The things that reasonable parents do.

I remember now. The night my son died, he cried out in the middle of the night. Some time around four, I think. But I was too much of a zombie. Something had happened and I was at work late. By the time I got to sleep, I just wouldn't wake up. Couldn't transition from the sound in the dream. But I knew he was crying. A part of my brain knew it wasn't the dream making those sounds, but I ignored the cries. I just wanted to get a few hours in. My wife was always a sound sleeper. She never even knew. When I asked her if she heard the sounds the night prior, all she could say was the same thing: "What sounds?" We were both hysterical when we realized what had happened.

Last night, the cries happened at the same time. Four in the morning. The same exact time as the night my son passed. Except last night, the cries ended early. Instead of half an hour, it was only five minutes. And then a pause. Silence. I thought something had happened. Maybe the cries would start if I turned on the monitor.

But the monitor was already on. Like I said, I didn't remember turning it on, but there it was. Glowing with the speakers crackling.

I took the monitor off my nightstand and I rested it on my chest. I gave myself a few seconds to adjust to the brightness. There it was. The dark blur. My son. Sitting up in the crib, looking at the monitor with the glowing eyes. There was no crying, though. We both sat there, looking at each other through the miracle of wireless technology. Through time and space. Through the crackling.

I tried to speak.

I couldn't find the words.

The dark mass stood up and seemed to slide over the railing of the crib and out of the frame of the monitor camera. Something was about to happen, but I kept staring at the monitor. I started to hear sounds coming from my son's room, just off camera. Whatever it was knew how to open a door, because the next thing I heard was the creaking sound of my son's door swinging out into the hallway. It wasn't a loud creak. Just enough for me to question whether or not I heard the door moving. Then the nightlight in the hallway went out.

I tried peeking my head over the edge of the bed, but staring at the monitor for so long had made everything else darker. I couldn't see it, but I could hear it. Something was there. I held my breath to see if I could hear it. I could feel the air in the room shift with the air conditioner. But whatever had been moving had stopped. Maybe it wasn't there. Maybe I was starting to lose it. Maybe my wife was right to be distant.

I took a long breath to steady myself. It was just the AC. Just the hallway light burning out. But then I heard something shift. Something was in the room, and it was resting directly next to my side of the bed. Everything fell silent. I couldn't even feel my heart beating. My eyes teared up.

I clicked off the monitor's screen and then I twisted the monitor around in my hands to use it as a flashlight. I moved slowly. I stopped breathing. I couldn't hear it, but I knew it was there. I peeked my head over the edge of the bed to where I knew it was. I pointed the monitor.

Half a breath.

I clicked on the screen.

I saw it before the screen had reached its full brightness. Rusty orange and night's gray blurred with the few rays of moonlight slicing through the blinds to color the plush face of a stuffed animal. The face of a fox with the body of a child. Glowing eyes of fire shot up from the edge of my bed and into my face.

I woke up screaming to my wife giving me CPR. My face was marked by a large, scabbed gorge.

—

The fourth week.

When I was a much younger man, being raised by my father, I was often told a story about a fox. My mother wasn't around often while I was being raised. She was there, but that was just her body. Her mind was somewhere else. My father was the one who raised me, and every year that I remember being alive we went deer hunting. Those have always been some of my favorite memories. Ones and zeros that have always stuck around and reminded me about the best days of my life.

Out in the woods of upstate New York, you could walk for miles without ever seeing a trace of man. Just the trees and the wildlife. The animals we were hunting would always be the last things we would ever see. The math involved in it all was amazing to me. The odds. The numbers. How long we would spend in the woods compared to the encounters with our prey, sitting in a tree stand, walking through to try and push the animals one way or the other.

It was when we sat in the tree stands that my father would start talking, always at a whisper. He'd tell me about the fox that he would see when he was a boy, same fox in the the same woods. The actual woods that we would be sitting in while he was telling me the story. He saw the fox for years and never understood what it was doing out there or why it always seemed to find my father. My father explained it in his own way. He would always say, "A fox never dies. Not really. You can tell when you look in their eyes that some are thousands of years old. They carry knowledge in those eyes. They're old. And if a fox finds you, they're looking out for you. Sometimes that's a reason to be worried. Most times, it means you're doing something right with your life."

I was never afraid of foxes, listening to those stories. I always thought they were lucky. A guardian type of animal. And as long as I was my father's son, I always had a stuffed fox lying in bed with me. The same fox I gave my son the day he was born. Same fox that was in the crib the day my son left us.

Most of the time, when we would finally get a deer, it would go down pretty fast. My father would give me the first shot and if I missed he could usually get a hit. We'd look out into the woods, climb down the tree and head over to the deer. Most of them died with their mouths open, so they could get their last gasps in. I was lucky to never have to watch the last breaths, but I could always imagine how it must have felt. How those final pulls of air didn't quite reach the lungs. The emotions that must have been within the mind of a creature that doesn't understand the reasons behind what has just happened.

I was the one who found my son that morning. I stood there longer than I should have, but I didn't need to pick him up. Not to know that look. The glossed eyes, the jaw slack with his mouth open.

He looked just like the deer. When I finally held him, he was as cold as metal in the snow.

Memories. The more we gather, the more they seem to attach themselves to objects. I look at a rocking chair, and I remember being a boy. I smell a flower, I'm reminded of my wife. I see a fox, and... well. There are a lot of things I think of when I see a fox. Just like last week. Whatever it was, I wasn't dreaming.

Life in the past week hasn't been easy. I've been waking up in my own bed again, but the nights are still the same. Every night, the baby monitor is turned on and I hear it. When it all first started happening, I tried to get my wife to go with me to a hotel, so we could escape and not have to go through it all. I even had the car packed, and she still wouldn't go. Wouldn't even talk to me. She had a blank look that I'd never seen on her before. She was staring at me like I was insane.

A couple of nights ago, the volume of the crying was unbearable. Even with that, my wife never woke up. She just laid there like a pile of pillows. Her answer to everything. Alice was always like that.

Cyn, I mean. My wife. Always wearing white.

Eventually, all came to a head for me. I decided to end it all, and spend the night in my son's room to settle everything. I brought the baby monitor with me and locked the door. I was going to stay there the entire night, no matter what happened.

I couldn't sleep. I just sat there in the rocking chair, looking around my son's room. The wooden toys, the polaroid photos we lined on the walls, the drawers of clothes, the table we used to change him on, and the crib. The empty crib. Midnight came, and then one and two o'clock. There was enough light from the moon to see the shadows of the clockface on the wall. When the clock came closer to four o'clock I stood up and held my breath.

The baby monitor turned on in my hand. I looked down for a moment and saw my son through the screen, standing there at the edge of the crib.

I started crying.

When I looked up, my son had the head of the fox with his eyes glowing. My heart started racing and I realized that I should take a breath. I took the air in slowly through my nose. There he was, the fox. The child.

The fox opened up its mouth and cried a loud human cry. I looked back down to the monitor and saw it was my son on the screen. I dropped the monitor and looked back at the crib, but the fox had climbed out of the crib and was standing in front of me.

I felt my nose start to bleed. My ears were on fire from an intense pressure. I knelt down and felt the weight of the world in my legs. My body wasn't mine. My son wasn't mine. My life was no longer mine.

The fox started to walk toward me, the eyes getting brighter and brighter.

I could feel the room shaking. My legs were numb from squatting down. I held my arms out to my son. He was beautiful. I closed my eyes.

Then it happened. He was there, in my arms. It was him. We stayed there for a long time. Until the sun began to rise.

I had to look. I couldn't stop myself. I wanted to see if the fox had left. But when I pulled him back to look at him, he was gone. There was no fox. No child. I was alone in the room. I stood up and my legs buckled. I started to shake, and that's when I woke up.

I woke up from everything.

I looked around. I was lying in my bed. My son's fox was lying next to me. My fox. I raised my arm and saw the IV stuck in me. It was my bedroom, but monitors were next to the bed. I turned to see if my wife was there, but she wasn't. How could she be? The room was bright. It was the morning. White walls, white ceiling.

Nurse Alice walked in. She always wore white scrubs, always clean. I made her tell me the truth. What had happened to everyone. My son, my wife, my father. She had a look on her face—how many times had she told me the truth?

That it had all happened years ago.

Hospice.

I was in hospice. My son had died decades ago. My wife had been gone for nine years. I had dementia and the moments where my lights turned back on were getting farther apart.

Reality.

It was just a moment. A break from the fog.

I'm just like the coyote, chasing that dumb roadrunner. Living every day the exact same. Repeating the mistakes. That dumb coyote. Always getting the anvil dropped on him. There was no monitor. No coyote. No fox. There was nothing. Just a bunch of ones and zeros buzzing through my head, confused as to the order they're supposed to stay in, mixing and matching to muddle up my memories. Just numbers floating around in an empty space. It's all in the numbers. That's how you understand anything of real value in this world. How many days did I have left? Did it even matter? Counting down to the end.

This story branches out from all of the books my wife and I read in order to prepare for our first child. We read all the stats and odds of every likely contingency. It was pretty interesting, but also frightening to read the realities of life. Mostly, I thought about how I would have never learned any of those numbers if I didn't actively seek them out. I was never told how hard it was to have a child, or how easy it was to lose one. Formal educations don't produce that information.

It was this whole unspoken aspect of society, and so I wanted to address it. It can be pretty scary being a new parent—no one wants to lose a child. But life happens. So I wrote the first part of this story, about the parents who lose their child, only for the spirit to still cry every night through the monitor. Through an accident, the first part was tagged when I posted it online. The tag said that this story was supposed to be part of a series, which meant that there should be a part two.

When I thought about it, I realized that I did have a little more to say about the father who lost his son. So I continued the story and I made it into something that I was and am really proud of. I am a pretty paranoid father. I stay up later just to make sure my sons are doing alright. Especially when we let them sleep in their own room.

I would find myself waking up a few times a night to check the baby monitor, especially with my first son. In many ways, I am the father in this story.

Checkpoint Charlie

Talking truck usually fires me up. I get excited. Or, I used to. Until yesterday, driving truck used to be more than a job for me, but sometimes, well, now, I guess I'm thinking about hanging it up. Getting out of the seat and behind a dispatch somewhere. Everything changed when I was driving near my old home last night.

A lot happens inside a cab while you're on the road. The Lord knows that. Sometimes you see the impossible. Everyone else on the road slows down, but you saw the impossible just the other day. It's just a work day for you, and anything can happen, anything can connect.

You're dodging the Bears and the Boy Scouts who are all trying to take pictures and give everyone invitations to the local courthouse. You're avoiding all the reckless Harvey Wallbangers, trying to prove how fast they can go. Or you're warning everyone in the convoy about the Willy Weaver in the granny lane, hoping he doesn't get picked up for some field sobriety.

Spending time talking on the tin can isn't just about dodging the Checkpoint Charlies, though. We aren't all just a bunch of middle school girls chatting up gossip. The tin can has its purposes. Sometimes you warn your fellow Aces, the Bulldogs and the Jammers, about the roads. The SWIFTies are pretty good about pitching in, too—even though they roll in slow motion. Maybe there's a gator from some guy's torn-up rubber. Maybe Bambi is out and about. Either way, you help each other.

Sometimes I get a little too chatty for the CB radio, and I find myself not using it. I'll mumble a bit. Not in the crazy way—I just sometimes find myself talking out loud. The radio is nice and most truckers use satellite these days, but sometimes it helps to just hear your own voice. I usually find myself saying much of the same things. We all have our filler words when we're trying to get some emotions out.

"Fricken Bear."

I was driving at a decent speed, just maintaining with traffic, but I still tensed up a bit. Bears have the power to take away your entire life. To them, it's just a traffic ticket. We're just a number. They love tagging truckers.

Now, don't get me wrong; my brother's a cop. But when I'm on the road and another man has that sort of power and it's me or him, I'm looking out for me. I have a load to make and a job to do. Sometimes speeding up a bit is just what I have to do to keep eating. I've spent most of my life on the road, so it's not like I don't know how to handle a big rig. Some of those younger Bears don't realize that, so I have to keep an eye out. It's all a part of the game.

Everyone on the road's seen *Smokey and the Bandit.* Even the Bears.

When it comes to a rig, you can teach anyone to lay down on a hammer. But there are demands, and getting the license and papers isn't easy. It's some heavy responsibility. If you're hauling over 80,000 pounds, there are a lot of other factors at work when you're on the road than what most folks think. Some of those tiny things on the road weigh less than 2,000 pounds. What do you think one of those look like if I get cut off?

Exactly.

Most folks don't think about stuff like that, though. Some decide to pass me going one mile an hour faster. And they're totally oblivious when they drive like bumper stickers. They pass me, anyways, and then they get off in a few miles. Usually, they make it to their exit about 10 seconds before I pass them up. I don't try and get all preachy all the time, but I do get worried. Most truckers worry a lot. It's in the job. You want to keep your papers. A fender bender doesn't look good when you're trying to keep your job.

Sometimes, it gets close. That Bimmer thinks they can make it and they just barely do. They think that a rig can just go from "go" to "stop" as easily as their little rollerskates. Brakes on a rig aren't the same as the brakes in your four wheeler. Rigs use air brakes. Like the systems that stop trains. Ever see a train stop on a dime?

Fricken exactly.

If the compressor isn't up to speed or something isn't being properly maintained, the air brakes might fail. Not only that, it takes time for the air to return to the system. Hitting on the brakes too heavy a few times in a row may mean that they won't reload. Being in control of something like that isn't an easy job. I haven't ever had to pull into one of those runaway rig ramps, but they're there for a reason.

There's a lot of beautiful things about driving a rig. You get to see your country. Sometimes you're on the road at a certain hour and you're all alone out there. You're responsible, doing a job solo. Your mind wanders, and you think of things. Of gadgets, girls, your life.

As a kid, I used to think about suicide and stuff a lot. I mean, I was clinical. I used to daydream of just stepping out in front of a bus or something. Don't take that the wrong way. I wasn't ever a really unhappy kid, I just thought about that stuff. Now that I drive a rig, I think about how crappy that would have been for the driver. There aren't a lot of jobs like this. Every day at work you play Russian Roulette with the public. One of them may screw up and inadvertently cause their own death by your hands. It's a strange job to have when I stop and think about it.

This sort of job can really put pressure on that family life of yours, too. I used to try to get home on the weekends. But after what my wife did to me, I just stopped going. I'd say something nasty about her, but she isn't worth it, and I just don't care about all that anymore. I was younger, now I'm not.

She was all sorts of wild, and she was barely out of her teens when we met. She loved the trucker lifestyle in the beginning, and used to hang around truck stops. That's how I met her. She liked the trucker gadgets and everything. She'd always spend my money on something new and crazy for my rig. She was sweet, for a time. The most impulsive and emotional girl I ever knew. She really did look so young and pretty the days we were together. Like the Lord Himself came down to shine on her pretty little freckled face. But I don't find myself thinking of her too much these days. That was over ten years ago.

I live out of the rig these days. It's not so bad. Sometimes I think back to my youth, and I see how far I've come. You save a lot of money when it's just you. Sometimes I drive near home, but I try not to stop. I never want to have to feel those feelings again, and if I saw her, I wouldn't be able to keep it together. But, I mean, I guess I just avoid it.

Like I was saying. There're definitely positives to trucking. I don't pay rent, I just pay for meals. I have an icebox and a microwave: life is pretty good. You drive long enough, you start making buddies. You seem to always need a piss break at the same stops. After a few years, you recognize the regulars.

There are also a lot of opportunities to help others. If I'm running early on a haul, I'll pull my rig over and help some stranger change a tire. The other day I helped a nice older couple with their overheated Type 2.

Easy.

Being on the road as often as I am, you see things, good and bad. Times when the trucker wasn't fast enough. Times when the brakes didn't stop a rig quickly enough. The civilians all slow down to see if some stranger died, and they speed away after they get enough rubbernecking in. I've been involved in a few fender benders. Everything slows down for a moment, and my heart stops every time. So far I've been lucky, but having those moments to experience harsh realities helps keep you in touch. Keeps you awake on the long days.

Sometimes a four wheeler stays on the left side of a rig for too long. If you have to swerve, those tiny cars on your side don't stand a chance. Other times they hug the bumper, as if that will affect the way you drive.

They just don't understand.

One quick moment or mistake leads to the road turning into a parking lot.

I'm rambling. I know that. Yesterday happened and that's that.

I was driving around where I used to live. Out by one of the major truck stops on I-95. I was on a long run. Had gone five hours straight in the same lane. A miracle. Then traffic hit. Not a lot, just the assholes. The types who pull up next to rigs going one mile an hour faster—the creepers. Sometimes they stick there for miles. Sometimes they pass and then slow down. But my brakes. If I use them up too much, they don't work right away. Like I said: they're air brakes.

A white four wheeler passed me and slowed down almost immediately. I was convoying behind a couple other rigs, so the white four wheeler had cut in between us. Like the guy was doing it intentionally. Another car just sat next to me, so I had to lay on the brakes to slow down all the weight I was hauling. I had a massive load of garbage—probably bananas.

The guy to my side got the hint and I managed to swing out into the fast lane so I could maintain speed. First thing everyone else behind me did? Try and pass the other semi on the right so they could cut me off. They all lined up to my right and the white car finally decided to speed up.

"Dammit, keep moving."

So there I was, stuck in the fast lane. And then I saw a rollerskate pulled off in the grass up ahead. On my side of the road.

It isn't entirely uncommon for people to pull off in the median, but it is a red flag. Truckers always see these things first, since we sit so high up. It gives us a chance to react, but at that point I'd hit the brakes so much from the right lane cars cutting me off that I was running the risk of not having any brakes. And there we all were, approaching the rollerskate pulled over in the grass, just a yardstick or two away.

"Come on."

It was past sundown. I had already made up my mind that I was going to go horizontal at the next truck stop. I was so close.

A lot of truckers have personal rules. Most of us will do all we can to get over a lane when they see a Bear with someone pulled over, or anyone else in the grass for that matter. But I was blocked in yesterday. And it wasn't going to happen. I was going to be passing right by the rollerskate in the median. The moment after that realization was the moment I saw the woman standing there. Right there on the side of her car. There she was, looking out down the lane. I knew exactly what was happening.

When you can see the accident before it happens, time slows down. Like something inside you knows this memory will stick, so your brain kicks into overdrive so you can remember every detail. I could smell my dip bottles, and I could count the exact number of headlights and eyeballs in my mirrors. I pulled on my horn long enough for it to run out of air.

"Fricken…"

The white car guy in front of me was able to swerve and missed the lady. But that's because the lady next to the road wasn't trying to be hit by the car. I only had a few seconds and when you are carrying that many lives on your back you need to make a few choices. The first thing I did was hit the brakes, but I knew it'd only buy a few seconds. I was in the left lane, there were several cars feeling my bumper out, and a few on the right that wouldn't even know I was coming over. And if I did move over, I'd take them all the way out to the trees. I weighed the lives.

I had to either risk it and test the crash test ratings of those four wheelers next to me…

Or one lady could die. Someone who already wanted it to happen.

"Jesus, help me for it."

Someone half naked and banged up, someone who had the look in her eye. Someone who had seen things and decided she never wanted to see them again.

Someone stepping right out in front of a semi that had just run out of air brakes.

My lights lit her up.

Her red hair.

It was a windy night.

Her eyes were wide.

I couldn't see her eye color, but her eyes looked right into me. Right through me and into the rig. She didn't see me, she didn't see the person she was forcing into that scenario. She just saw her emergency exit flashing red.

She looked so young when the light hit her face.

"Fr..."

I swerved as much as I could while still staying in the lane. If I pulled into the grass, I could have gone into oncoming. I had done everything I could. I'd pulled every emergency lever and pushed the buttons.

But it was just a moment. Drivers have these rules that we follow. Where we try to avoid situations like that, because we never know when it could happen. People these days. They step out in front of trains, they jump off buildings. They pop pills in hotel rooms. People never stop to think of the poor guy who has to clean that up, or the woman who finds a body on the cement. Sometimes it's a child who finds a body like that.

"Fri..."

Impact.

No one survives that amount of trauma.

A lot of gore happened in front of me in that moment, but what I saw, clear in the light, was her cell phone. It came right up to the window and cracked the glass.

"Freckles..."

I managed to stop a bit down the road and I called the cops. They had me park where I was and we all met at the spot where it happened. No one else stopped besides me. None of them. Just another Saturday night for them. They all slowed down to look, though.

"She was so young."

I stayed and filled out the paperwork. Official looking people took pictures. I took some for the insurance stuff.

Called my company.

The cops were somber about it and my company told me to sleep in a hotel on their dime for a couple days. This morning I pulled into a car wash and spent the day wiping that poor girl's dreams off my rig.

I got the call this afternoon.

I was the girl's reported next of kin.

"Impossible."

It was Mindy, my ex wife. It was Mindy standing there in the middle of the road, her red hair blazing in the lights of the truck, half beaten up, probably crying.

"Oh, God."

She'd been raped after her car broke down. Just a couple guys in a pickup truck. Some guys acting like they would help her. No one else stopped to check on her.

"Christ..."

The whole thing happened, and Mindy called her mother to tell her. Mindy was still on the phone when she stepped out in front of me. The last thing she told her mother was goodbye.

Jesus, forgive me.

There's nothing else to say.

My father spent a year or so as a trucker when I was in high school. He enjoyed it for what it was and liked the experience, but eventually decided he wanted to move on to another job. A big reason for that was the average driver he would encounter on the road. People cut off trucks as if trucks are able to stop as quickly as cars can.

After seeing so many instances of truckers killing drivers who didn't know any better, my father decided there was too much risk for himself in the position. I've always tried to remember those lessons. I let trucks in and I'll be that guy who leaves the gap if a trucker's blinker is on. They hold a lot of responsibility in that job, and I respect that.

Jolene Jolene Jolene Jolene

Jolene is dead.
She was the greatest thing in my life.
And I loved her.

—

I went through quite a lonely spell as a younger child. It is possible that I never grew out of it.

When I was much younger I used to be constantly transfixed by the birds that took residence near my home. I was the type of child who enjoyed being by myself in the woods or sitting on a back porch watching the birds. When the weather was sour, I gazed through the window to the edge of the wood line outside the back of our home. When I did happen to turn on the television, I was held captive by the nature channels. It was an utter obsession, and the birds took the center stage of my life. Meditating on those years, I would have to say that they were the most emotionally fulfilling of my life.

I was birthed by a single mother and she chose to raise me with a rather absentminded parental approach. A child should never be the source of strength in a relationship between the child and the mother, but that was very much the dynamic my mother and I had. I would not have traded it for the world, but I do sometimes wonder if being forced into maturity so early was the proper path for me.

The times I would be allowed to spend with my mother were very precious and we always were able to enjoy each other and our laughter. My mother was the one who introduced me to the knowledge of birds. She would spend hours telling stories about each type of bird and why they were all significant. Then she would be off to work again, and it would be several days before we were able to spend more time together.

There were no surrogate fathers in my life. My mother appeared to have been celibate, save for one night. I had few friends throughout my schooling and never maintained contact very well, especially as I grew older. I was never picked on or tussled with. I was simply the child who was there. Recesses involved sitting and observing.

The beauty of birds is that they are always present. There are very few places on this Earth that do not have some form of bird attempting to remind us to look up into the expanse.

The thought of flying was extraordinary. I yearn to know what people must have thought before human flight was feasible. I still often wonder if even then humanity took for granted the gifts of the birds. While I was in constant awe of the miracles birds could perform, it was their fraternity that most attracted me to them. Several species of birds mate for life, just like dolphins, or the way we like to think of humans as doing.

The most beautiful times of the year were when the migrations would occur. I once read a story saying that when a goose is worn down with age, the dying goose would be accompanied by two of its friends on the journey to the ground—even mid-migration. The dying goose would lay down, and while it died its friends would remain for comfort and protection. Whenever the migrational season would come, I always looked for the geese flying in small groups. If I saw three, I would always wonder if that was a final flight, and if I saw two, I knew that there was a goose somewhere on the ground that would never raise its wings to the sky again.

The thought of a goose never dying alone touched me. Often, when I was lonely, I would visit the story in my mind. A final flight seemed romantic in many ways. I would always wonder what feelings had to go through an animal's mind when it knew its moment had come to fall asleep for the final time.

I was rather young when I realized the wisdom of birds in relation to death. I watched birds all of my young life, and I had never seen one simply fall out of the sky. They would glide back down to Earth every time. I realized that birds must always recognize the moment when death is upon them. They face that moment with dignity and grace. They know when the final descent is, and they don't attempt a last flight when their time has arrived. I respected that stoicism.

In the window of my youth, there was always a beautiful white pigeon that would dance in my yard. Of all the birds I had ever admired, she was my favorite. Pigeons and geese have always been glorious in their own right. Often overlooked, and ever graceful.

If you take the time to observe nature, you will eventually be given the gift of photographic moments. Birds defending their nests in my backyard. Birds discovering their mates for the first time. I was privy to a front row seat in the circle of life. My window was open to everything I would ever need to understand about Creation. I learned about sex at that window. I experienced my first death through that glass. I had gone into a trance and been sitting there for hours. I remember that I felt as if I could almost feel something leaving when the bird fell down off that branch in the backyard. The bird did not appear to be about to fall. But it did. My favorite white pigeon.

I thought of the story of the geese, and I ran to be with the pigeon so it wouldn't die alone. I had often daydreamed of actually touching the white pigeon, but in that moment, when I was finally able to hold her, I wished I had never felt those desires. I had nightmares about the eyes of the bird. After thirty minutes, the eyes glossed over and the twitching stopped. Sometimes I can still vividly recall her flying.

—

She was the greatest thing in my life.
And I loved her.

—

Holding a loved one in their final moments is the most tragic sensation I have ever experienced. Years after holding the white pigeon, I was present during the death of my mother. We had been arguing about something trivial. She was lecturing and I had allowed myself to fall into a trance of indifference, as if I was staring her down from my mental perch, high in the trees. The regret I've held from those moments can at times be overwhelming.

My mother started shaking and screaming and she let go of me with a push when I tried to see what was wrong. She was looking into my eyes, unable to blink. Her knees caved forward and her body twisted while she fell to the ground.

I attempted to be closer to her to help. Anger passed, and the moment between me being angry and becoming scared was the swiftest change in emotions I had ever experienced. Every time I tried moving closer to her she pushed herself back further.

My mother continued shaking and screaming, crouching down on the floor, her gnarled hands moving over her ears. I didn't understand what was happening. All I knew of life were stupid stories about birds.

At some point my mother stopped shaking and there was a moment between her and I. When you're the child you never have to be the source of strength. You're not supposed to be. But you do have to be from time to time when it's just the two of you. I squeezed her hand while we both cried. Hopefully she knew I loved her, but in the moment the words weren't there.

The doctors later said it was something with her brain, something about a cavity and pressure and extraordinary circumstances.

The longer I considered everything, the longer I realized that there was another possibility.

—

Today is when all of the events of my life came full circle. Jolene and I have been living together for years. Today, Jolene was being a little more frustrating than I was used to and I had hit my wits' end with her. She kept repeating herself and repeating herself and I could not stop myself from simply staring at her.

I tuned myself out until Jolene started shaking. She fell down in her cage and I had to scoop her out so I could be there for her. I did not realize what I had done until after it was too late.

It had always been *me*.

I've sat with Jolene all day. And I think I have found a way to escape everything. Maybe my gift won't just work on animals and people. Maybe it will work in a mirror, and I will not have to be alone. I will take with me my memories of Jolene, my mother, and the days when I knew the joys of companionship.

Loneliness is an aspect of the human condition. We don't seem to be built to be alone. Sure, sometimes it feels good to get space for ourselves, and a few people need the loneliness to be happy. I don't judge that. But I know I need other people around me to feel fulfilled, and when I feel the most lost, it's because of my physical isolation from others. Some people find that animals can fill the void just as well as people, and I think that's beautiful.

The goose story is from the writings of Dr. Robert *McNeish—specifically a short article called* Lessons From Geese. *The information included has been researched and as far as I know it has been verified by the scientific community. I say that because when I read something like that, I want it to be true, as it's one of the best examples of sacrifice that I know of in the natural world.*

Hush

I woke up today at 4:30 in the morning, the same as every day. I hit the snooze button three times, then stared at the clock until I felt the cool touch of my two dogs' noses on my mouth. The signal that I had to take them out. I knew my wife was awake, but it has been some years since we have both gotten up together.

There once was a time in our relationship when she would take the batteries out of the alarm just to mess with me. She would change the times so that I woke up an hour early. She made sure I was never late, but we used to have fun, usually at my expense. That used to be us. It isn't anymore.

I came back in from walking the dogs and picking up crap just in time to make it into the bathroom after my wife had finished up. We slept together, lived together, and still managed to barely speak to each other or spend time in the same room. It was mostly work, at first: our schedules just never lined up. After a while, however, work just became the excuse.

It was as if magic slowly transformed the house every day. As soon as one of us would turn around, the other would switch this or that on, open those curtains over there, start cooking that part of the meal. I always turned the coffee pot on, but I was never the first one to grab a cup. We were both living separate lives. At some point in our marriage we stopped sleeping together and were instead simply sleeping in the same bed.

This morning I brushed my teeth, sat on the john, and rinsed off. Bathroom time has always been a private time. A time for meditation and a chance to wake up. I have always woken up half an hour before I have ever needed to, just so I can take my time in the bathroom. Janice always rushed to get out so we never had to be in there at the same time. It worked well. Even when our marriage was great, we never spent any time in the bathroom together. No brushing teeth, no washing hands. We absolutely avoided it. Some friends of ours would comment on how this practice seemed odd, but those relationships all ended in divorce and ours endured. The way I looked at it, spending too much time together was just as bad as spending too little.

Every three days was a rotation for food. Pancakes, scrambled eggs, bagels. Same three meals. I never complained about it, but breakfast had been just like every other part of our marriage: rehearsed and repeated.

I don't know how any other marriage would have been for Janice. I always was predictable, much like all the other men in our town. I held a nine to five job, followed all the sports when their season came around, drank two beers a night at dinner unless it was Sunday night football or card night. Average, and stable.

If I compare myself with the other men I have met, I am certain that they would have faced the same as me if Janice had married them. Women were all the same. Janice's emotions were what let the marriage fall to where it was. She used to act differently, like she knew what she wanted. Back when we were dating, love felt like a game without rules. Anything was possible before the structure of a long term relationship set in. When we got married right out of high school, we were two kids playing grownups. We substituted youthful exuberance for worldly experience. It was silly, it was great, it was American.

These days, all the mysteries that made our early games worth playing have largely been solved. I know exactly how to make her happy. I know what her perfect day is. Her nightmares. What I can do to get under her skin. None of it bothers me any. Instead I feel almost a hollow feeling when I think about really putting forth the extra effort. Maybe that's how I've changed.

Janice came from a rougher life than I did. Her parents weren't the perfect inlaws, and we rarely visited with them. She was left alone a lot as a child and never really spoke about it. Seeing the way she grew into herself, I figured she always enjoyed being alone. She needed the space, so I gave it to her.

I'm about five years away from retiring from my first profession. I rarely think about work while I'm there. I mostly daydream about the next steps, finally going out to get the job of my dreams, with a pension under my belt. That extra security will really help with me continuing to build our garden in the back yard and I also won't have to hold my cards so tight on card night. I've been on autopilot for so long that it comes easy now, and Janice is the same way. She makes breakfast for the five of us in less than five minutes, cleans the house by noon, and watches TV until the kids come home. Sometimes she helps them on homework. Sometimes she just fixes up dinner in five minutes and she'll keep watching TV.

The American Dream. I go off to work, she raises the kids and keeps up our home. The perfect life. I told her a long time ago that I didn't want her working. We have always lived in the same old-fashioned town and playing by old-fashioned rules has been important. Sure, she had a few things she wanted to do, but then we had kids, and life changes with children. Not in a bad way—she was always happy. She really was.

Today I came home and kissed Janice on the neck for the first time in over three months. Maybe the last kiss was Christmas. In any event, it had been quite some time since we had been intimate in any way. It was brief, though. She had to take care of the kids, who had started to get sick a couple weeks ago. Janice took them all to the doctor and got some medicine that the kids had been taking, but it didn't clear anything up. If anything, they got a little worse. The blessings of having children.

So, I came home, ate dinner, and sat down on the couch to take a breather. The kids came to say goodnight and Janice took them upstairs to bathe them and tuck them in. They were a little old to take showers together, but they still insisted on it and so we never felt like stopping them. Some sort of bonding thing.

At least it saved water.

Weird kids, but I loved them. That's what you're supposed to do. We would go camping on the weekends when we could and we'd leave Janice at home so we could get some bonding time in: fishing, watching sports... Dad stuff. The kids had their quirks, like all people do. Janice was always insistent on not coming. She enjoyed her alone time.

I didn't spend too much time downstairs. I could tell Janice was making the extra effort and I figured I would try to make an extra effort or two myself. She had cooked my favorite meal, and didn't leave any dishes for me to clean. I could see all the vacuum lines in the carpet and the countertops were wet from the rags she used to clean them up. Perfect night.

I lit a couple candles and waited in the bedroom for her to finish up with the kids. She was always pushing me away. I thought that I would take the initiative for once. Be the man of the house.

I hadn't seen a look of surprise on Janice's face like that in years. It's funny how things like that seem to not matter until you experience them again.

Then you wonder why it was never a priority.

I knew it had been a rough couple of weeks for her. We ended up showering together for the first time in our marriage. I don't know why we had always avoided it. There was something deeply intimate about lathering each other up, sharing the water, trying to keep each other from getting too cold. It didn't take much encouragement for either of us.

We didn't even leave the shower. It was beautiful. The spraying water forced us to both keep our eyes closed, but we knew each other's bodies well enough. We used half a bottle of body wash cleaning already clean bodies, over and over again. We took a break only to move to the bed, and we didn't even bother toweling off.

The pleasure of that emotional warmth had never felt the same with anyone else, and it never would.

Is it possible to fall in love over time? To grow to love a person? Why not? So many secrets, but how many of those were actually secrets? As it turns out, none of them. You end up learning everything about a person. Everything, eventually. Hopefully before it's the end.

Janice was crying.

I was always of the opinion that a person should marry their best friend over a romantic interest. You fall out of love, you fall back into love. There are the beats of a relationship, but you two move on. If you marry for love, you'll get your heart run over. That's why Janice and I could always take breathers. Get our space for a few months and then go back to each other. Because we were friends before we were partners. That matters.

Those breaks gave us moments. Real moments where we would connect and let it all go. Just forget the problems and we would be more than friends. We would reconnect and remember the reasons we dated all those years ago in high school.

We held each other so close. Janice knew about the secretary five years ago. It was OK. I told Janice I knew about the drinking. I forgave her. She told me about the foreman; I already knew. It was a one-time thing. Janice told me she loved me more than anything. I told her I would always love her. I would always be there for her.

We kissed for a long time. Like we were dating again. Kids. We were always just kids trying to figure out how to play grownups.

Then, under my lips, Janice started to buckle. Her lips tightened and I realized something was wrong. I didn't want to believe it at first. She used to always joke like that, joke just to show me how much she liked me.

I couldn't believe something was actually wrong.

She just kept saying that she was sorry. Over and over. She started spitting up blood and talking about fire. She wasn't saying anything that made sense. I tried holding her down so she wouldn't hurt herself. She flailed a lot. I grabbed a phone, but she had stopped moving by the time the operator picked up.

Why.

Our bed was a mess. An enormous pool of blood and dinner. The smell of stomach acid and whatever it was that Janice had drank to make herself go through what she had gone through.

Poison. She had done it right in front of me.

I held her until the paramedics arrived. She couldn't be pronounced dead there, but I knew that she was. But that wasn't the most horrible part of the night.

No, the most horrible part was finding the kids.

I first wrote this story five years ago during this amazing upsurge I experienced immediately following college. I had gone from living in the barracks of the Academy to living in an apartment where we were allowed to have alcohol. It was amazing.

Army career paths are dominated by gates and boxes to check. Upon graduating college, officers commission and then have to go to training so that they can become a general expert on their new field of work. Infantry guys go to sleep on rocks for six months to a year before they're sent out into the world to drag their knuckles on the salt of the land. Armor guys sleep in tanks the size of small apartment buildings—they own grills, hook up water coolers, and generally have it good in those giant RV's (these are jokes; their lives are not as luxurious as I depict, but we like making fun of each other in the Army).

I was an artillery officer. So I went to artillery school to learn about putting rounds (many of which date from the Cold War) on targets. We did math. Lots of math. Calculating things like precipitation, wind, rotation of the earth, trajectories and arcs and stuff that made us go cross eyed. In the movies, they make canons seem like a stick-your-thumb-up-after-licking-it sort of art form. Nope, you silly human. Artillery isn't that at all.

There are numbers and calculations and there is repetition. Joking aside, the repetition of regular Army life can occasionally make people lose sight of the importance of living life. To be brief in my explanation, this story came a bit from that fear that I would ever let any system overpower my desire to live a life worth living. Even a system as great as the Army.

Soul Sucker

I have to admit that I wish I was a little more informed when it came to being a new mom. I never paid attention in health class, and I definitely didn't care about books, before or during the pregnancy. I didn't attend any birthing or breastfeeding classes. Like I always had, I figured that would all click; like it always turns out, it didn't.

Who needs advice anyway? Not that I'm a ton older now, but having a baby matures a girl without help from anyone else. Besides, none of my friends were anywhere near ready to have babies of their own. I'm kind of younger than I probably should be, but this is my life and I made the decisions that I made, so please don't judge me for it. I'm proud of my experiences and I'm proud of my little man.

I was a total party girl, so the father could have been many guys. I drank to get drunk and blacking out at the parties was something all of us did. I'd usually end up at home anyway. I never judged the guys for what they did. I probably asked for it. I'll do just about anything when I'm drunk and I know I was putting it out there. I could have stopped whenever I wanted to.

I say that big talk about partying, but there was a moment that made me figure I should stop. I live in a pretty big city with a hot underground club scene. I went to house parties whenever, but I also would go out to the clubs and see where I could end up. The last one I went to wasn't the best place to black out, but it was ladies' night and they were handing out dollar drinks. There was a pretty big gothic vibe there: lot of black, lot of organ music.

I remembered dancing with a man named Hanz. He was tall and blond and gorgeous in that *Twilight* sort of way. There were a few other guys, and the night was fun until I had slammed a few shots at the bar.

I woke up soaked in an alleyway, like I had been scrubbed down for something. I smelled like rubbing alcohol and I had hickies all over. That was kind of a rock bottom for me, not that it mattered: after a month, I missed my period.

Women have been giving birth forever. If they could do it, why couldn't I? It was a little more complicated than that, but I made it through it and I'm a better woman for it.

I'll walk around the city to do errands, and I'll bump into my old friends. I try to avoid them if I can because I can see the looks in their faces. They're always telling me that I look too thin, that I don't look well. I tell them I stay inside so much because of the baby. Everything about it is embarrassing: someone I think of as a friend judging me, asking me if I want to go out when they know I can't leave my baby.

Sometimes I bump into Hanz, which is weird and super awkward. The baby could totally be anyone's. Hanz is always nice about it, and we have a kind of weird friendship going. He seems to enjoy checking up on me, which I'll admit feels kind of nice. Hanz even named my son Franz. Said it was a traditional name where he comes from.

Maybe Hanz is the one. There's worse things that could happen.

Franz finally has his teeth coming in, and I'm a little worried about that. I don't want to go into the details of what they look like, but my nipples are scarred from Franz sucking so hard. Harder than I thought a baby could suck.

Today was especially bad. Franz usually cuts me a little when he feeds. Sometimes I think he wants more blood than he wants milk. He sucks up most of it, but I feel so light-headed afterwards that I get worried that I might drop him if I pass out too soon. And today, he cut me pretty deep.

I saw spots and closed my eyes, only to still feel dizzy.

We woke up on the floor and the carpet was stained.

I was still bleeding a little, but thankfully the cuts started to block up. I looked over at my baby and he just smiled at me, his face covered in blood. I cried for an hour in the isolation that only a single mother can ever know.

I'm trapped with the greatest joy of my life.

The greatest roadblock to any life I could have ever lived.

Tortured with love, and bleeding from the most fragile part of myself. When I was younger I let my breasts define so much about me. Like they really mattered in my social life. Now, my breasts are weights chaining me to the constant reminder that I made a mistake.

My wife and I recently had our second child and I'm not too surprised that a lot of these stories center around children, being young, or what it feels like to be a new parent. I guess I just feel more inspired with the events of my own life and want to interject a little of that in what I'm writing.

My hat is off to the women who can do the breastfeeding thing. You ladies are stronger humans than I am.

Having a creature (don't get me wrong, I love my sons) attached to my nipple, knowing that the creature has teeth and could bite down at any time completely freaks me out. I couldn't do it. Especially the way we oversexualize breasts in our culture. It feels like a dirty bedroom experience combined with a horror movie. I'm entirely supportive of breastfeeding. I just couldn't do it myself.

Good Time Charlie

So there I was, draining another dive bar, talking to the over-forties. I had my sights on a patron or two and I played the place well enough. They weren't friends this time, so it was easier. The question I had to figure out was which one of them was more sober than the other.

There was a time in my life when I went for the guys who were stone-dead drunk. Something about the power made it worth my while. The drunker they were, the more embarrassed and ashamed they were in the morning, especially if they were over thirty-five. They almost always tried to scoot me out of their place as soon as possible, which was alright by me.

These days, the sober ones are the better picks, because then they can drive, I get a place to crash, and they're usually cool to drive in the morning to drop me off at my car.

I do the rounds in my state. I try to never drink in the same town twice. I don't even really have a job. I'll just let you in on it: I sell breast milk. Huge market for it. Over two dollars an ounce in the right neighborhoods—I usually ask for a dollar, though. I have one of the automated pumps that plugs right into my car, gets me the ounces I need, and then I scope out Craigslist to see who wants to buy any in the nearest city. I make the sales and move on to the bars. Find a guy, get some action, get a bed, usually get breakfast. You should see how many numbers I've gotten over the years.

Back in the day, society used to call them wet nurses. Women who were perpetually pumping out milk. It's rare in the Western world now, but breast milk is still a commodity. Not to get too into my past, but I had a stillbirth. Very late term. It was an awful experience, but my milk came in anyway. The guy I was with liked it, so I'd pump and keep the milk around. Eventually the relationship fizzled out, but by that point I was selling the milk.

You name a personality type, they buy my milk. Weird high schoolers who see something crazy for sale on the Internet. Single moms. Creepy old men. Scientists. Creepy young men. High school coaches. Creepy chicks. I try not to be judgmental about it. I'm not the type to deny anyone anything like that. Besides, who knows what those types of people are normally like. Everyone gets caught up in a moment from time to time, and we tell ourselves so many things to make our actions acceptable. I know that.

Some parents are actually totally responsible about the transaction and just want some milk for their newborns. Maybe they had a C-section and the hormones didn't all work out. Money is money.

So, another night in a bar. After a few successful transactions, I figured I'd go home with a loner last night. So many different types of guys at that age are trying to pick up young twenty-somethings, it really is just easy to look past the shamelessness of it all. Who knows what I'll do when my looks start to go.

Some guys scratch their noses, some say a word over and over again, others just stare at your rack. This guy cracked his joints. All men have tics. Especially when they think they're about to get laid. This one couldn't stop himself from cracking different joints on his body. Neck, fingers, back. He would go through each in that order while he would be talking and every time, something would crack.

His name was Jerold, but I only half pay attention to names. Guys like lying about stuff like that. They think I'm out to ruin their future chances at being the president or something if they give too much information, when, really, I'm always looking for the same thing they are: just a few hours of fake love and a nap next to a stranger.

Jerold lived in a trailer out on a decent plot of land. He had one of those creepy driveways where the trees were covered in Spanish moss and the branches clasped together over the dirt road to create a tunnel. Those types of roads have always creeped me out. But a bed is a bed is a bed.

Jerold had his head on straight and we didn't have any of those awkward moments once we walked in through the door. Right away he threw a beer in my hand, got a bottle of liquor out, showed me the ice and he turned on the shower. A man after my heart.

We drank, we showered, we hit the bed, the kitchen table, the stove... you know the routine of a wild night like that. We were on the stove when I realized his truck lights were still on. At least, that's what I thought they were.

It was pretty hard concentrating. I was drunk and we were messing around pretty heavy. Jerold's body wasn't toned, but I've since learned that holding out for the pretty boys doesn't always give a girl a place to sleep. I wasn't exactly in the frame of mind to care about his body or the headlights for that matter. But they were out there. The blinds weren't even shut. We rolled around and knocked over a bunch of utensils from one of the counters.

Time passed; Jerold kept going at it. Every once in a while I would hear what sounded like water flowing, but maybe it was rain running off the trailer. I tuned back into the sex.

Everyone wants to feel good.

Rain is just rain.

We were on the ground when I realized that the headlights weren't white anymore. They were a bright yellow. A warm yellow that seemed to flow over everything. I looked up at whatever-his-name-was and that's when I really noticed something was different. He wasn't the same man I'd hit on at the bar. In the bright yellow light, I could see that he had no more whites in his eyes. Just black glass. And he was holding me. On top of me. Inside of me.

He leaned in.

I started to hear thick cracks as Jerold arched his back. It sounded like he was cracking every bone in his body. He finished with his spine and then did his neck. He then opened his mouth and his jaw seemed to pop. I looked at his chest and saw that his ribs were cracking and his chest seemed to be expanding, as if he was able to flex and move the bones of his body.

Then Jerold grabbed me, hard, and pulled me in. I could feel other parts of his body cracking. The parts that were inside me. Expanding and moving in unnatural ways.

"Don't go. I'm almost there. Don't you want me to finish? I know I want you to," he chuckled.

I did all I could to push him off of me. To get him out. To get him out of me. That's when I realized that the yellow light was fire. And that the trailer was starting to burn. I reached around for anything, something. I felt the edge of one of the knives we had knocked to the ground. I cut myself trying to pick it up, but I got it and I pushed it into the man's stomach.

He didn't make any noise. Just an exhale. He slowly got off of me and stood up. It was as if I had just stabbed a sack of sand, because hard chunks of gravel seemed to be spilling out of his abdomen. I scrambled to get up and ran out of the building to the lights. I could hear Jerold begin to crack his body.

He was reshaping himself.

I didn't even stop to find any clothes. I ran out of the trailer and toward the truck. Only there were several trucks out there. I turned to the trailer and saw it surrounded with emptied gasoline cans. I felt sick and threw up.

I looked up from the vomit and saw the man standing inside the kitchen, in the window. Looking out at me. I couldn't see his mouth, but I heard what sounded almost like a train coming from I don't know where. A scream so inhuman that I couldn't do it any justice. I looked at the trailer in horror. Someone put a blanket over me and I passed out.

I wasn't the first girl Jerold had done horrible things to, but I was the first to survive. The townsfolk were going after him, not me. I just happened to luck out by choosing Jerold on the same night the rest of the town decided to barbecue him.

I want to move on physically and emotionally, but something's wrong now.

It's not a hangover.

I tried pumping this morning, and nothing came out. I dried up overnight. That's not a thing that's supposed to happen. No one just turns their milk off like that. I should at least be leaking, but I have nothing.

What really worries me is what Jerold said right before I escaped. That he wanted to *finish*. What if he had? Because my stomach feels knotted up. My stomach doesn't just hurt—it feels like something is inside of me, growing.

See Me. Let Go.

It wasn't a dark alley, or even behind a bar. The first time I was stabbed was on my way to my car, in one of those supercenter parking lots.

I wasn't one of those types you're thinking of: the gangbanger, the hoodlum, the wannabe tough guy. Just a regular person, with no enemies, a few friends, not in the greatest shape, but the guy who once knew his way around a football field. I was a normal guy.

Still am.

I was never very good about getting my keys ready in time to get into my car. I always waited until I was at the car door to fumble for them. That night was no different as I heard the quick thump of footsteps behind me. Someone was running. I turned just in time to get tackled. I curled my head up so that my back took more of the blow. I learned from football that no one wants ground contact with the head when they're getting knocked down. At least not when they aren't wearing a helmet. It doesn't matter who you are, a blind hit will take down anyone. Even Houdini couldn't take all the hits he saw coming.

The wind was knocked out of me and I felt that desperate pause. The pause where the brain attempts to assess whether you're dying or not, whether you should go into high alert because you're not breathing. I was on my back, and I could see my attacker. I held a hand up and I tried saying something, but I couldn't breath yet. I tried coughing to reset my lungs.

I managed a stutter, then a deep inhale. My head got fuzzy from the sudden rush of oxygen.

I looked up into the stranger's eyes. A blank slate, no emotions. His pupils were dilated and appeared enormous in the heavy yellow light from the evenly spaced street lights scattered throughout the parking lot. He looked down at me, but I never felt like he was actually looking at me.

Just through me.

There was a book I read when I was thinking about joining the Army called *On Killing* and it got pretty deep. It talked about soldiers and the difference between killing a man up close and far away. Up close is harder because your victim is right there, screaming at you, and you feel all of the emotions that might elicit. There's reasons fighter pilots and bombers don't have as many instances of PTSD as the guys on the ground doing the work with their hands.

That book taught me about a lot of aspects of humanity and parts of myself that I knew I didn't want to tap into.

The military wasn't for me. It wasn't that I was against any of it, I just wasn't the type that would excel in that environment. I was one of those long-haired neckbeard types. I was in shape for football, but that didn't mean I wanted to make running my life. Don't get me wrong about the neckbeard hipster comment, either; I had a beard way before it became the trendy thing to do. I'm not the type to use that as a political statement. I have a beard because I enjoy it and I hate shaving. There used to be a time when a beard was just a masculine thing to do. A beard can be a lot of responsibility, after all: checking every time you sneeze, making sure you eat carefully.

When you're trapped in a situation of such uncertainty, your mind goes to strange places. A hand was on my face, and all I could think about was how worried I was about my beard.

Looking up at the man, a bit dazed from the wind being knocked out of me, I didn't know what to say. My mind stopped wandering and it started to focus. I was afraid. No shame in admitting I was afraid.

I never saw the knife. I just remember the man throwing his hands over his head and me instinctively knowing what it could be. What it ended up really being. The way he had his hands in the air, I could tell he was holding something. I blocked my face and got ready to protect myself.

When the man brought down his hands I managed to grab one of his wrists. Then I had both wrists. And I saw it, a knife. Slowly being pushed toward me. It didn't matter how much I pushed back, the man had the weight of his body leaning into his hands, pushing closer to me.

It wasn't my first fight. I had gotten into a few fights back when I played football. It was a part of growing up for me. The one thing about fighting is that anyone can win. Just like anyone can get tackled. Anyone can get stabbed. The man smelled like a gym floor. As strong as I was, I could see the knife and I could feel the weight slowly moving down. It was happening so slowly that it felt like I was the one about to stab myself.

I felt the sensation of electricity suddenly flow through me, like my central nervous system skipped a beat. I felt nothing, at first, but realized that the man's hands were pressed against my chest. It took me a second to realize the knife was pressed deep inside me.

I was screaming.

The man just sat there on top of me, looking down at my chest. That's when the fire lit inside of me.

My nerve endings started to lose the numbing electric sensation and replaced it with the feeling of pressure and burning. I looked up at the man and he moved his eyes to look up to my face.

And I snapped.

I put both hands on the man's biceps and pushed. The knife slowly scraped its way out of my body. What happened next was really fast. I knew I was shaking, and I knew I was on top of the man, and I knew my shaking was uncontrollable.

My mind went on hold.

I wanted to breathe; I wanted to live.

I wanted revenge.

Survival.

Anything.

Not death.

Not for me.

Not that night.

I fell next to the man. Survival.

It took forever, but eventually an ambulance came.

The man was so bad off after I finished with him that he was taken away first. As I laid there, I felt a renewed appreciation for soldiers. For killing. A renewed appreciation of the human condition. The random experience, and the emptiness after the whole ordeal.

The police did all the work. I spent a few days in the hospital, but that was it. I didn't lose my job or anything and when the cops released me they told me everything they knew. The man wasn't anything special. Just a vagrant with a few charges here and there. A man with a history of mental illness who chose to be homeless. There wasn't much else.

Sometimes, that's the worst part of the entire experience. That there wasn't a reason. That I was just there. The wrong place at the wrong time. The guy probably didn't even do it for money. He just wanted to kill me for the hell of it.

I was never sent to jail for what I did, and I eventually made a full recovery. The cops said it was in self-defense and I didn't have any time to have a motive or plot or do whatever it is that makes people guilty of contemplating the way they're going to defend themselves. What sticks with me the most is the emptiness of the entire experience. The worst thing a person can do is kill, but because of the law, I was just let back out into the world.

I didn't ask to be.

I didn't ask to be attacked, either. I was just there, and then I was on top of a man and he was dead. No ceremonies. No real acknowledgement of my actions. Of what I endured. The vagrant never woke up in the hospital.

Sometimes, at night, I'll wake up in a sweat and remember everything. In my dreams, it will all play out. Events are always different, but the face of the man never changes. Neither his cold, slack expression, or his total comfort with what he was trying to do.

I've seen stabbings so many times on the big screen, I had always wondered what it was actually like. I usually find myself wondering if the actor put a lot of research into the experience of being stabbed, or if the director or writer knew anything about what they were creating.

So for this one, I did a lot of reading to make sure I understood a little more about what I was trying to talk about. The idea of a random confrontation becoming an experience like this really struck me.

Lady Macbeth

I'm recording this on a tape recorder. Might as well…
I'm sorry, can I start over? Yes, of course I can. Ok.
I'm being recorded using a portable tape recorder. I'll do my best to say it all…
It just sounds forced when I say that line. I'm just going to start.

—

I am a guerrilla writer; the type that goes into the weeds of a story and comes out of the brush with the truth. Like Woodward and Bernstein of Watergate, or Seymour Hersh of My Lai Massacre fame. The herald of honesty, I always acknowledge the dirt that no one wants to admit exists. The layer below the surface holds the secrets of humanity that are the most interesting. That's the real way to write. Total fidelity. My book about soldiers was intricate in diving into the lives of young men and women during the current wars. If I held on to my desires for anyone to continue to take me seriously, I could not very well burn all those relationships by writing something that the soldiers couldn't be proud of reading. I didn't taint anything with opinion and vitriol. I stayed true to the source, and found the perspective. The secret is in the jokes, the humor. The humanity is in the humor, in the hyperbole and metaphor.

My last project was my magnum opus. I wanted to speak about the homeless, so I became homeless. You might hear me describe that and assume I was just another hipster writer, attempting a barely unique angle on a tired theme. Well, I took it seriously and spent a year in the gutters and filth. An entire year. I extracted my own cavity-riddled teeth from my mouth. I consumed rats and garbage off the streets when threatened with starvation. I pushed the limits of humanity and came out the other end with perfection. Non-fiction gold. And a few worms.

I could only outdo that sacrifice with a greater sacrifice. Where my life as a vagrant was a sacrifice of the body, I have now attempted the greatest sacrifice of all: that of the mind. I have seen war and crime. But murder? Murder was not an experience I was intrinsically prepared to endure, and so the challenge was worthy of my efforts.

Self-reflection was to be a key part of the endeavor—I needed reality to speak from my prose. If I could write of the sacrifice and endurance of soldiers, of the resilience of men living in alleys, then I could write of the killer to expose the killer in all of us: the universal human experience of life and death represented by the man capable of taking a life to give their own life fulfillment.

The killer I chose was named Clarissa. I never learned or cared about her last name. She was a specter of a person, a shell, an anomaly in the modern times of constant surveillance. One day passed, and then another, as days have always done. Then, suddenly, Clarissa appeared at a local police station to hand herself to the authorities.

Fifty-seven murders.

She had proof.

No one knew her age; she appeared to be in her forties. She wore glasses, but the more I considered everything, the more I was unsure of her need for them. The overall look of her was motherly. There was something warm about her eyes and her demeanor. I initially believed it was a sociopathic type of behavior, but I've grown to believe her smile was genuine. She enjoyed smiling.

I initiated my research with books. I never blindly jump into a subject. I consume everything I can before ever considering the physical portion of the project. I read about killing: about serial killers of the past, their methods, information about the police and detectives who tracked and apprehended such individuals. I attended night classes at the local college in order to understand the detectives and the theories and the like. After I knew enough about the more standard crimes, I began researching the details of the exotic: books on cannibalism, mutations, and medical information on cadavers. A true guerrilla writer can enter the mind of their subject, become them.

I began having nightmares every night. That was when I knew I was ready to meet Clarissa. I would meet her for one hour at a time at the institution in which she was being held, every week, for eight months. In the beginning, I was afraid of her. I would leave those encounters and head straight for the water closet so I could vomit into the toilet.

Clarissa was something else. A creature with human skin. All of her personality traits were otherworldly. The way she shifted her eyes, the way her jaw moved slightly side to side when she finished speaking, the stillness in her hands. She felt absolutely no regret for anything she had done. I can freely admit that I developed a level of respect for her because of that. She was strong in ways I was not. She didn't need to live other lives to feel whole.

I did.

I needed the lives of others to approach feeling whole. Clarissa was who she was even when everything was taken from her. She took those other people's lives and did with them what she wanted. Instead of playing pretend, she fashioned her own world. Not a book, but a real place. Real events.

What made Clarissa so extraordinary was that she didn't fit into any of the normal categories in which female serial killers are often classified. Even the most evil women throughout time have killed through impersonal means. Some female serial killers have others do their work while the women function as a Lady Macbeth. Others use poison. Actually, many have used poison. Very rarely does a woman serial killer use a gun or a knife. And even more uncommon is what Clarissa did.

She would use her bare hands to rip her victims apart while they were still alive.

It takes less than ten pounds of pressure to rip off a human ear. The same amount of pressure can be used to gouge out an eye. Eye gouges are more technique than anything else. And with some practice and form it is simple to break an arm, pull it out of the socket, and then use a pair of fabric scissors to snip off the skin.

Those are the conversations Clarissa and I would have. She would never smile during the somber retellings, but I could hear how much she enjoyed recalling them for me. She was evil and confident. Her connection to all of the crimes she claimed was easy to follow: she would eat the bodies and keep enough of the bones around to prove her actions. On more than one occasion she kept the victim alive so she could feed the victim their own fingertips. One finger a day. And Clarissa was proud of all of this.

In the beginning I could not endure the full hour before I would have to excuse myself. I would kneel next to the water closet toilet and sometimes even cry. The things she was capable of and she was human. In my dreams I saw so many things: I would dream about Clarissa and see her doing the actions she talked about. I could not understand if she was the worst of us, or if she was just a representation of us unvarnished. A part of all people that we never talk about. The part of us that gets angry and wants to kill a driver that cuts us off on the road. The part of us that sees evil and wants it gone. The part of us that watches TV and sees what fame is these days. Clarissa appeared to have tapped into the part of man that I was always in pursuit of: the truth below the truth.

If I were to be completely honest, I needed this book. More than anything else. My history as a successful author is more or less defined not by my ability to sell books, but by my personal satisfaction with my writing. That has worked well enough in the past, but I haven't sold as well as the publishers would like me to. If this book doesn't succeed on the lists it needs to be included on, my publisher will cease to do business with me.

I was sent a letter addressing my books and their inability to garner public acclaim. An official letter, marked and re-marked with stamps and postages and signatures and the scent of those cold cubicles that I never wanted to return to.

More dedication.

More force.

I needed to get this book sold, and I still need to tell Clarissa's story, my real story, the story of humanity.

Then and now.

I needed it to get out there and to mean something to the world. To the famous people and to everyone else. I needed to be known and the only way to do that was to enter Clarissa's mind. To really know her. To stop throwing up my fears and to swallow them.

Roughly two months ago, Clarissa began to truly warm up to me. She ceased her attempts to make me gag and began talking about deep aspects of herself. I saw the real her, and it was *truth.* Real honesty. Real humanity. She had an ability to remember each scenario in such detail—she was perfect for a writer. She had prose, she had poetry, she was Kant, she was Fitzgerald, she was Hemingway, she was Nixon for my Watergate, the Monica to my Bill. Clarissa slowly walked me through the events of her life.

Clarissa was easily one of the smarter individuals I have met. She thought through almost everything I ever saw her do or say, and she spent just as much time planning her murders. She utilized random selection in regards to her victims. Locations were arbitrary and scattered across the country. Her only consistent requirement was that her victims were all either children or several decades older than her. It didn't seem to say anything really about her, other than that she always picked victims who were physically inferior to herself.

Because of her methods, no one ever thought it would be a woman in her forties that had done all of those killings, while traveling across the country.

Her genius came from her boldness. Clarissa was the only reason she was in jail. In fact, her evidence was mostly circumstantial. She knew the killings very well, but she didn't seem to have any physical evidence. Just a total understanding of the murders. Really, she could have posted bail any day she wanted to. She just chose not to post bail. She wanted to be there.

Clarissa would tell me in one moment that there were bones everywhere, and the next meeting she would say there was no physical proof. She once told me that there was a trail to get there, how to reach what she achieved. She never mentioned how to find the trail.

Oh, the tape is getting low, would you like for me to flip it before…

—

Alright, continuing.

We had been talking for a few months. I had felt very odd for a couple of weeks—angrier, more easily irritated. The way I found myself looking at people also changed. I felt superior in every way to everyone around me. I *was* superior. I had learned so much about myself and the rest of humanity. I had the secrets I had always wanted to have. And the things I had been dreaming about... they should have felt like nightmares, but I started to gain a sense of purification from them.

It wasn't long before Clarissa was telling me things I needed to hear. The real secrets to the methods. Disposals. Selecting targets. Superiority is addictive: hard to kill off and constantly insatiable. Recognizing that within myself didn't change my need for the behavior.

I found myself tailing people in my car. Watching the rest of the world differently. Seeing the people for what they were. Everyone was a senseless mole, burrowing around the dirt, blind to the sun.

I eventually understood Clarissa's need to kill. The sensation of power was supposed to be greater than the emotions and hormones attached to orgasm—that's what the books had said when I did the research. For the type of person that Clarissa is, killing is a form of self-realization. Her way of finding fulfillment. Writing this book has allowed me to see that. To feel that. There is something terribly profound and beautiful in the painful struggle of humanity.

My first murder was a drunk. He never made it to his car, and no one ever saw me do it. I'll write down the address of the bar some day just to prove it. I felt true life and I was a power beyond man. My life was defined by death, which gave my life all the more meaning. All the more weight in the universe. I was a god of destruction and a being of life.

So many men and women come into the world and replace their parents. They have children who replace them. It will take hundreds to replace the impact of me.

The final day I met with Clarissa, the world was different. I was able to finally see things from her point of view. From her eyes, everything seemed to click over and make sense. I could understand what she was thinking and I could see the beauty in her choices. I felt more relaxed than I had been throughout any of the other weeks and months.

That was my moment of self-actualization. Absolutely everything was clear, her methods and the things that the detectives missed. I had to keep talking so that I could make *her* keep talking. I knew how to find her trail.

It was the way she looked at me. That disconnected stare. I realized it was more than just a mental disconnect. Those glasses she was wearing? The ones she didn't need to wear? I wondered who the last person to wear them was, and how Clarissa squeezed the life out of them. It was her twist. The one thing she did to let the universe know it was her.

She didn't smile with her eyes, but I knew with the sound of her voice when we said our goodbyes that she could see I had finally understood. The last thing she told me was that she liked my glasses. It meant something.

It is interesting what a person will do at home once they learn that their savior just killed herself. It was all over the news that night. I couldn't avoid it. Clarissa didn't just end herself, either. Not a boring death, but a marvelous one. It must have taken her forever to get her jaw unhinged, but once she did, she was able to fit her entire forearm down her throat. It must have been beautiful.

I killed five people that night before the police finally found me and realized my truth. Five men who deserved it in their own little way. Five men with glasses.

I was glad I was caught. Glad I was found. Glad I get the opportunity to share my accomplishments with the world and the beauty of it all. I became a pupil of Clarissa, of my Creator. My God.

Now I am given all of the time I need to finish writing. I am fed.

I am allowed my privacy. I have even spoken to my publisher. They were hesitant, but once I told them what the book was about they could not resist my final masterpiece and testament to my Creator.

Alright. I suppose that's the time limit for the week, yes?

I'll see you next week, Jennifer. Let me know how the book is coming along. I'll enjoy reading it once you're done, and please let me know if you want any of my notes on Clarissa. I'm finishing up my own manuscript on the events. Here's your recorder back.

I'll help any way I can. Us girls have to stick together.

He Only Had Sex With Strangers

He only had sex with strangers.

That's what my father used to tell me when I asked who my mother was. He would tell me that he never really knew her, that one day a woman he had probably slept with just left me there.

I was my father's penance. He totally accepted me in his own way.

And I accepted that. I didn't grow up particularly unhappy. I thought I was pretty average, socially. Don't get the wrong idea from all this information, though: I loved my father. More than anything. He wasn't ever perfect, but I always thought of him as a man to look up to. I grew up worshipping him. The moments we spent together lasted forever, in good ways. Sometimes he would grill out in the back and we would just have dinner. The two of us.

I enjoyed the time together because school wasn't much of a party. I would go and be invisible. Talk to the girls, talk to the boys, finish talking, go about the day. Teachers never really saw my hand if I ever raised it. I was just kind of around. I was never made fun of, but I also never made it into any of the cliques. Never wanted to play a sport. Never wanted to get into computers. I was just there, existing. Maybe that was the one failing of my father. He never pushed me to do much of anything. So when the time came for me to decide to do something, I'd often choose option two: nothing.

When I was younger I went through a night terror phase where I'd hear the oddest sounds in the house. If he was there, he would eventually come into the room and make sure I was alright, then tell me that they were just dreams. Just sounds in my head, mostly yelling. And with that, he would explain them away. Most of the time, though, my father came home late, so on those nights it was just me. I'd wake up and sometimes I thought I could still hear the sounds of my dreams. I was always so scared that I'd never leave the bed. Then I would just wake up the next day and it was as if nothing ever happened. No more screams.

We lived in an alright neighborhood. It looked like the type of area that had a lot of break-ins, though we never had problems with that. Everyone in the neighborhood looked after each other. Our house was a single story, and as far as I knew, it was the only house on the block without a basement. My father told me that's how he could afford to buy the place when he was younger.

Behind our row of houses was a pretty large sandlot. My father once told me that the city owned it. It was historic in some way, so nothing would ever be built there. There used to be an old mill or something and, at some point, the city dedicated a monument back there. But that had since been forgotten. After so much time, it was mostly just a dirt lot. Dirt and a water tower, which sat directly behind the house. On some nights, when the screaming in the dreams was bad, I would climb up the ladder of the tower and hang out up there. It was one of the older towers. I wasn't even sure if it was still being used or not. Sometimes I'd play around with it. I was pretty sure that if I really wanted to, I could just use some of my father's wrenches and open that thing clean up. I would daydream about being Moses, unleashing the next great flood to clean the neighborhood, parting the seas of debauchery and laying claim to the new vision of the world. When I was smaller, I used to keep a wrench up there, just in case. I probably wouldn't ever really do it. I wasn't a total narcissist or anything like that.

For the most part, I was an indoor kid growing up. Our backyard was filled up to either side of the fence. It was mostly disorganized piles of trash, with one or two paths that had been trotted clear over time. Not exactly child-friendly. The only time dad or I would go out there would be when we fired up the grill. Sometimes I would worry about us setting some of the garbage on fire, but dad always seemed alright about it all.

Our neighbors all seemed nice enough. The only name I knew was, our next-door neighbor, Tom. Tom liked playing loud music from the 80's. If there were ever to be a soundtrack made concerning my life's story, it would have to be those 80s songs I heard every night of my childhood.

We didn't live in a particularly large city, and every road was littered with stop signs. Every single corner. It was a strange place, looking back on it. It was also only technically called a city. Most often, we called it the town. It was a border town at heart. The kind of place people would go to escape their lives, and the kind of place people would leave in a heartbeat.

There were residents, but we had a lot of drifters come through, too. No one ever really knew when people would just up and leave town. Especially the women around there. They were always chasing after the city guys that would drive through. Sometimes my father would take me to a diner or some other restaurant, and by the time we went back a few months later, it was as if the whole staff had been changed out. It was always the women, though. The men seemed to stick around the town their entire lives.

Sometimes we'd be at one of those restaurants and I'd hear the voice of some random woman and her voice would pervade my night terrors for weeks. Every time I'd wake up sweating, remembering her face and I'd hear the echoes of the dreams. It unsettled me. It was probably also why my father wouldn't take me out too often. And I never blamed him for that. I knew I could be a little embarrassing.

He was such a blunt man, my father. I knew he was out late with a woman most of the nights he was raising me. He was never one to hide things from me. And if I would ask, he would just out and say the answer to any questions I ever had. I learned a lot of things at an early age because of his lack of boundaries.

I guess my childhood could be summed up as an understanding between my father and myself. I had my life and my father had his life. We both lived there, and we both tried to help out around the house. Growing up with him was like having a roommate. The older I got, the longer we both just spent our free time in our respective rooms. I was always a quiet kid. I had a small footprint and did the invisibility thing at home just as often as I did at school. I thought of it as a game. Being able to open and close all the doors in the house, move around, walk anywhere in that place and not make a sound. I thought of it as my superpower. If only I could really turn invisible. I often think that could have solved everything for me.

I started to question this social contract with dad in my teens. Living a childhood like the one I lived, I was partially raised by television. Television was a window to other lives, and by the time I was thirteen or fourteen, I could pretty clearly see I wasn't in an average situation. I didn't lash out or take advantage of my situation the way I'm sure most other kids would have. But I did wonder why our world was the way it was.

Of course my father being who he was, completely answered everything I asked.

"Why is it just you and me?"

"A woman dropped you off here. You know that. I never really asked any questions when she did it."

"Where'd she come from?"

"Not sure. Never knew many of the names of those girls back then. When someone moved away, their phone number changed. Wasn't like today where we keep the same number or have cell phones. She moved away, and I never saw her again. You've asked this all before."

"How many women have you had sex with?"

"Oh, I've long since lost count. I don't like to count, but when I stop to think about it, probably a few hundred."

"Why do you sleep with so many?"

"I don't know. Besides you, I don't really have anything else. I never got into sports. I never got into hobbies. I just kind of existed, you know?"

"Do you love me?"

"Well, I suppose I love you more than anything else. I keep you around, right?"

And that was that. A few years passed by and I never had a real reason to get any deeper into it. My father never struck me as the manipulative type. He was just a man, getting his rocks off and going to work every day.

Still. I was a teenager. I don't know why I needed to feel wanted. There was just something in the hormones that made me want to feel like I was important. Something more than a throwaway. Love defined me at that age. My father's methods of acceptance suddenly weren't good enough for some reason. I wanted him to accept me on my terms and by my definition of acceptance. In retrospect, it was a *bit* narcissistic of me. But teenagers are sometimes like that.

I started getting into the habit of staying up until my father would get home from his nights out. I was the closest thing he had to a wife. I suppose it was the young woman inside me trying to be some sort of maternally benevolent person, like I had to worry about him. I couldn't even sleep until I knew he was home. At first, I would get so tired that I'd just pass out from exhaustion. But once I was worried enough it wasn't as hard to stay up. It helped that I could always listen to my 80's soundtrack. Tom never knew it, but he kept me company on most of those nights through his music.

Around the time I was sixteen, I finally decided to stay up late and follow my father to whatever seedy places he was going to get laid. I guess I was just interested. Maybe a part of me wanted to see the type of place I could have been conceived in.

I wanted to get a glimpse of the type of women that were my father's type. Get an idea of who my mother might have been. I needed ways to define myself. For some reason, those women he was sleeping with seemed like a way to understand who I really was. After all, I knew my father better than any other man. If I could understand what he liked in a girl, maybe I could break out of whatever existential dilemma I was in. I was going to finally take some initiative. I could change the world, myself.

When he left the house that night, I figured I could keep up on my bike. With all the stop signs everywhere, it took just about the same amount of time to pedal a bike around. His first destination was a place that I figured was a strip club. I hung out across the street and waited for a while. It didn't seem like too long, maybe half an hour, before I saw my father leave the building from a side door.

He had a woman with him that dressed like a stripper. I saw them walk to his car. Twenty minutes later, the stripper left the car and went back into the club. It looked like she was in a hurry to leave. My father was a little grabby when she tried to get out, but he probably also had a beer or two in him.

My father sat in the parking lot for a few minutes. I wasn't too sure what he was doing. Maybe that's why he would come home late. Maybe he just sat in parking lots drinking. But then another woman came out from the strip club. A young brunette who got right into my father's car. She also dressed like a stripper.

I don't know what I thought about the whole situation. I assumed that my father would continue on into the night. Maybe he'd take the girl somewhere, maybe he just would stay in that parking lot. It wasn't even close to the time that he would normally arrive home.

The next thing my father did was head back toward home instead of going further down the town main street. And he had the new girl in the car with him. It freaked me out a little. He had never gotten home that early. I didn't want him to catch me not being at home. I followed his car from a reasonable distance, but when he approached the turn to get to our house he kept going. Pulled into the old sandlot behind our house.

He turned his lights off once he made the final turn, and he coasted into a spot at the far end of the lot. I was lucky that the moon was almost full, because I could see my father get out of his car and walk the few hundred yards to the rear of our house. The girl was with him. I saw him go through the backyard and that's when I decided to sneak back into the house through the front door.

I had no idea what my father could have been doing. This didn't seem like normal behavior. If he was going to sleep with a woman in our house, I would have heard something after so many years. But he had never brought a girl home.

I was still good at keeping quiet, so I ditched my bike on the side of the house and I quietly walked through the front door. I wasn't sure what I would see in there. None of the lights were on. I thought I could hear some sounds in the house, but I couldn't tell. They were so muffled that I thought maybe they were coming from a neighbor's house. It sounded like it could be the bass to one of Tom's songs. I paused for a good couple of minutes. The longer I listened to the thumps of the music, the more I realized that the thumps weren't from the neighbor's music. It was coming from somewhere inside the house.

I made my way to my room first. Nothing had been moved around. I had gotten away with spying on my father, and he would never have known. But I was curious. I was interested in knowing why the night was playing out the way it was. And I wanted to know what the sounds were.

So I crept out of my room. I checked out the kitchen, and then the living room, and that's when I saw it. The rug in the hallway to my father's room had been pushed to the side and there was an open trap door there that led to a basement. The closer I got to the opening, the more I realized that the sounds were coming from there. I could hear whispers, and I could hear muffled sounds. I crept closer and closer to the door. I realized my breathing was getting a little out of control, and my hands were tensed.

When I looked down there, I only did it for a second. But I saw my father. I saw him swinging something and I could hear a thud that sounded like two pieces of meat slapping against each other. I got scared and went back to my room. I wasn't really sure what I had seen.

The next morning, it was as if nothing had happened. When I looked out my window, my father's car was parked in the driveway. Breakfast was normal, and school was fine.

When I got home from school, all I could think about was the trap door. And the basement I never knew I had. I stood for a long time in the hallway and I looked at the floor. How many times had I walked over the thick shag rug and never realized what was down there? Years. My entire life.

I started grilling outside. It was a nice way to stay peaceful. The coals were cold from the night before, but some were still good, so I mixed them in with the rest of the bag and tossed it to the side of the grill on the pile of hundreds of other bags that we had stacked up over the years. I daydreamed a little, but I was mostly consumed by the trap door. My entire life. I never knew.

I decided I was going to look. I had hours. The timing was right. I moved the rug and opened the wooden trap door. I immediately smelled a mixture of perfume and urine. There was a wooden staircase that I carefully descended.

I tried looking around from the bottom of the stairs, but there wasn't enough light. Then a sudden flicker and the sound of a match strike made me wheel around to see what was behind me. My bare feet felt the chill of the basement floor. It was much cooler down there than the rest of the house.

There was a woman there, in the corner of the room, sitting. She had a match in her hand and she was lighting a candle. She wasn't the same girl I had seen my father with the night prior.

The woman was chained down to what looked like a working toilet with plumbing. There was one of those cushioned seats on the rim. From the size of her legs, it looked like she hadn't stood up in years. She wasn't completely naked, as a single blanket draped over her torso covered her, for the most part. Her hair didn't look very healthy. It was so long it touched the floor.

"What are you doing here without Harold? Oh, do be careful, dear, you don't want to step in that puddle over there," she said. The basement seemed to warm up really fast.

I looked at the ground and saw her. The brunette stripper from the night prior was laying in a large puddle. It looked like blood, but it was so dark I couldn't tell. The stripper moved a little. She was alive. I knelt down to see if I could help her in any way. She needed a hospital.

"No no no no, don't touch her, she isn't done, yet. Harold and I still have some business with her. But soon, soon she will. Oh my sweet... honey? Oh my, it's you. I knew. Oh, baby, you're beautiful. This is it, this is finally it. Come here, oh, finally, come here and hug your mother. So, so you're finally eighteen? That's when Harold is going to... oh, bunny, don't look at me like that, come here. *ComehereandI'llshowyouthatIloveyou.* Forever. No. Please stay, don't. Don't do, don't call the police or do something like that. Honey, it's all alright, this is fine, this is good. He loves you. He loves you the most. I know this can. Look. Don't you. I love you. No, please *staystaystaystaystay*, come back and love me and it'll be... *comebacksoIcanloveyoucomebacksoIcanloveyouyoubitchhedoesn'tlove-bitcheslikeyouhecan'tloveyoulikehelovesmeyoubitchyouslutbitchI'lldo-youtooI'lldoyoujustlike...*"

I had to get out of there.

I didn't want to move the girl, but I couldn't just leave her down there. I ran over to the stripper and picked her up. She had bled a lot, but I didn't think it was from any major wounds and more like a lot of smaller ones. She managed to walk with me and we hurried up to the house.

I let the stripper sit down and dialed 911. I was in the kitchen. The phone was ringing when I turned to look in the backyard and saw the fire. The grill had caught half the backyard on fire. The house was going to catch soon and everything was going to burn up. I had enough time to scream into the phone that I needed cops, firefighters, guns. I threw the phone down and ran to the stripper.

I managed to get her out front and made her climb up onto a neighbor's car across the street. The house was already on fire at that point. With all the back yard trash, everything would burn.

I ran around the neighborhood to get to the sandlot. I climbed up the water tower. I needed the wrench to be there. I needed to save my house. I needed to save everything. I needed to finally do something. Do something right. Do anything.

The wrench was there and it was the right one. The perfect one.

I thanked my childhood self.

I started turning bolts. I got three out before the tower started shaking. I didn't need to undo a fourth. I started to climb down and felt the entire structure shaking. As soon as I made it down the ladder the tower burst. Water started pouring out and toward my house. It was a flood.

It wasn't until later that I remembered that the woman in the basement was still down there.

My mother.

Tom was the one who came to comfort me after everything. He was a few years older, but we ended up having a lot in common. I needed that.

A lot happened in the next year. The lot behind my house ended up being full of graves. And after some genetic testing, the woman in the basement did turn out to be my biological mother. The only woman my father had ever kept alive. I stopped trying to figure out what the lies were.

My father never came home from work that day. Maybe something triggered it, and maybe he knew I had seen.

I haven't had a night terror since the day I went down into the basement.

Laughing At Lunch

Before assholes started to crack down, you used to be able to order anything off the Internet. *Anything.*

Jess was one of those girls who everyone knew they shouldn't mess with... but it was fun to anyway. It wasn't that she was tough. But if anyone was going to go off the deep end and shoot up the school, it was Jess. Every school has a few kids that everyone thinks will freak out one day and pull a Carrie. Jess was that kid at our school.

Jess wasn't an ugly girl; she was actually pretty in a lot of ways. She was going to grow up to be one of those tattoo chicks, probably. She was just too weird for us back then. No one paid attention to the weird girl in school.

I was never the one who directly made fun of Jess's, but I'd be lying if I said I wasn't there and a part of it. Jess being the lowest on the social totem pole meant I couldn't be the lowest. My high school was like *The Lord of the Flies*, but without all the bloodshed. It was an emotional war. Most of the teachers just let it happen, too. They saw it all as schoolkid drama. Some probably thought it built character. Other teachers probably just wanted to keep their jobs and not rock the boat.

I don't think any of us really hated Jess. If anyone did, though, it was Dani. Dani was the most popular girl. Not only was Dani pretty, but she also made good grades, so the teachers really stayed out of her hair. That, and she had boobs before we did, so she would act like she was more mature than us. Looking back on it, I guess it was dumb how the age you had your first period seemed to matter. Girls.

Dani was pretty cruel, but in a lot of ways, she was right. She only said what everyone was thinking. We all knew there was no way Jess could pick locks; that she didn't know karate or any of the other wild things she claimed she could do.

Jess used to also talk about living overseas in the Middle East. We always thought she was a pathological liar so we never believed her. Jess would start telling these crazy stories in class or in between breaks and Dani was the one who called her out on them every time. Every single time. Dani would frequently cross the line, no matter what. It could have even been a true story. Sometimes, Jess even made some good points with her stories. That didn't matter to Dani.

One time Jess stopped a class to talk about camel spiders. She talked about how they could jump five feet in the air and would run after people. She made them sound like the facehuggers from the *Alien* movies, laying eggs in people's skin. She said that she didn't know what they were really called, but that everyone called them camel spiders. She said that whatever they were, camel spiders were different things from the spiders she had. Everyone seemed to not pay attention to that last part.

Dani was too busy saying how full of crap Jess was, but I heard it, and I made sure I was a little more careful around Jess. Having pets like that at home kind of freaked me out. I've never liked spiders, and if there was a chance Jess was telling the truth, I wanted to make sure I wasn't on the butt end of some of the possible insanity. I even said hi to Jess a couple of times in the hallway to try and be nice to her. She never said anything back, but her eyes would get a little warmer. I felt pretty bad for her. She never smiled.

The next day, Jess was being ragged on for talking about her gun collection. Dani was making a point of talking about how it couldn't actually be a real collection that Jess owned, that maybe her dad owned some guns, and that Jess should stop lying all the time. Dani kept going, too, and it got pretty deep. Deep enough for the teacher to actually make Dani stop, which never happened. I looked over at Jess, and I could see the fumes.

—

One weekend around tenth grade, Dani decided to have a sleepover. We let Jess know about it but we didn't let her come. Dani was pretty cruel about it, too, inviting a few girls that weren't even really in our friend circle.

We did silly girl things all night. Dumb stuff and a lot of talking and sharing experiences that half of us made up.

In the middle of the night, I was getting up to go to the bathroom when someone put their hand over my mouth. It was Jess. She was dressed in black and motioned for me to follow her. This was going to be it: she had finally snapped. She was going to shoot up everyone in the house, and I was going to be the first one to get what I deserved. We walked out into the hallway.

"Listen, I'm really sorry about everything. Everything, everything. Like really, really sorry," I whispered. I was still sleepy, and my brain wasn't working as well as I wished it would have been.

"Shh, I know. It's alright. Hey, you should go home. Right now," Jess whispered.

I looked at Jess for a moment and I realized she was serious. I was going to have a second chance. Jess was going to kill all of the popular girls in school. I didn't even consider stopping her.

I then realized that Jess wasn't carrying any guns on her. Instead, she had a shoebox that seemed to be moving. I could hear the scraping sound of pencils against the cardboard. And that's when I realized what was really going to happen.

You could buy anything off the Internet in those days.

I started to leave and right before I turned the corner I saw Jess slowly push the shoebox into Dani's bedroom.

We were in the middle of the lunch room a couple of weeks later when the first cluster of spiders burst out of Dani's skin. I got up from the table and couldn't stop backing up. Everyone in the entire school saw. Everyone paid attention to the popular girls in school. And there they were. All of the popular girls. Screaming and brushing their hands over their arms and the rest of their bodies as frantically as possible.

The only other sound came from the other side of the lunch room, where I saw Jess laughing.

Maslow's Hierarchy of Needs

After drowning for the third time, I decided I shouldn't go swimming anymore. There was no splashing or flailing the way TV always shows it. There were no screams. It is a horrible experience, drowning.

—

The first two times it happened, I was really young. I haven't been able to remember those experiences beyond the feeling of being in a black tunnel, with the shadows closing in around me. But the last time, I was in grade school, in a pool only a few feet from my parents.

We were swimming near the deep end and the pool we were in had ledges and steps where it got deeper. There were no ramps in the pool.

I don't remember how it started. I just remember being close to that ledge.

Then, my feet were suddenly not touching anything.

Maslow's Hierarchy of Needs. Everything else disappeared.

I didn't have time to speak. By the time I got my mouth above water, I exhaled as quickly as I could and tried inhaling, but the opportunity for air had passed. I needed to get above the water. I tilted my head back to kiss the air, but it wasn't there. Just a stained glass version of the world above. It reminded me of the standing mirrors my parents had throughout our home. Most were heirlooms, which meant they were cracked and broken. They couldn't show anyone a true reflection of the world anymore, just as the water couldn't deliver me the life I was losing.

Underwater, I would vomit. I needed air. My arms were entirely useless and weren't responding. They just kept flapping, trying to get me above the surface. The flapping wasn't splashing—it was a slow, rhythmic swaying. An uncontrollable, slow motion. My own body was killing me. I had never felt so helpless and desperate. I would have done anything for more life. I was supposed to be playing, I was supposed to be having fun in the…

I remembered the first times I had drowned. I remembered smelling my first rose and breathing in the sweet spring air of my backyard. The first time I rode a bike. I remembered a special I had seen on TV about drowning. A couple hundred years ago the approved method of resuscitation was blowing smoke into a victim's anal cavity from a portable bellow device. I was lost inside my mind, without…

Every once in a while a word would flash through my mind. A single moment of clarity where I could control a thought. Except the word or the thought, or whatever it was, wouldn't mean anything. It was just a word. A random moment. A last effort from a dying mind trying to make sense of an experience. Feeling totally abandoned. Random thoughts, random words, tangents just hitting me…

Objects in mirror are closer than they appear.

A breach. A moment above the floating.

"Air!"

Just a moment, my arms hurt from the push, and I had been so deprived of oxygen and had so much water in me that I couldn't inhale. I had to exhale first. I felt like I was inside a creature, a force of nature that knew full well what experience it was forcing onto me.

I slid under. Without enough time to breathe in.

More water.

Coughing.

"Wait!"

Gagging.

"Stop!"

My eyes burned from the chlorine. I wanted to cry and add a few drops to the body of water.

There was no light, no screaming. Just fear. And no one watching me could tell what was happening. Drowning was a silent affair. I even managed to make eye contact with one of the adults on one of my brief moments above the water. I just kept seeing the words and useless memories—I had a compulsion and a desire to not die, but the feeling was forced away by the immediate present. At that point there was no time to consider whether or not that moment was the end—it simply was.

"Don't."

Cry.

I wasn't experienced enough to think to kick. My body was on autopilot. My arms kept flapping and eventually started to climb a ladder that wasn't there. After one last attempt to get above the glass, I was under.

I once read that someone believed that drowning was the most peaceful way to die.

It isn't.

"Look."

Everything just moved in closer and closer.

It was horrible. I lost complete control over everything. My life, my body. I was stuck on a sinking ship. I had become a rock trying to break the surface of a stream.

I was down there.

"Deep."

My body, still moving, but with no hope of making it to the surface. I had to get somewhere, anywhere.

"Into."

A life preserver, the arms of a stranger. Anything.

The top of the water was now…

"Mirror."

A reflection of what life used to be. And I was on the other side. Stuck peering into the window to life.

"Abyss."

There was no personal reflection. There was only the struggle. The increased desperation. The random thoughts looped into repetition.

I saw the black after I had been under about a minute. At first it was in my periphery. Just a sensation.

"Is."

Just out of reach.

But then, it started to come in from the sides. Two enormous black masses.

The black was creeping in over my shoulders. Like a curtain of silk. I could almost see through the edges. The edge of life and death. I looked around the edges of the darkness, at the legs of all the other people living their lives.

"Waiting."

Then I looked back into the deep end. The edges of the darkness were like curtains rolling around my vision to form a tunnel. My body was still thrashing wildly. But, then, in the corner, something dark was separate from the curtain. Down in the deepest part of the pool.

Something was…

"There."

My body stopped struggling. This was it. The panic was over. I was going to die. Maybe there would be a light, maybe...

The tunnel started shrinking. My eyes grew heavy. There was a sensation that the curtain was coming from behind my eyes, from inside my skull. And my head started to fill with air and pressure.

I found myself staring at the dark mass at the bottom of the pool. It was a blob at first. But, as the tunnel pulled itself around me, the blob formed itself into something that could stand. It both stood and floated there at the bottom, expanding and contracting like the breaths I was incapable of producing.

It stood at the bottom of the deep end and stretched out its hand. I suddenly had control over my body.

I don't remember if it had eyes, but I knew it was looking into my soul. The abyss returned my stare. The tunnel was small, just enough to see the face of the mass. I felt a pulsing pressure inside my forehead that tickled its way to my spine. I saw a cloud in the shape of a hand outstretched toward me. One by one, I started to feel each of my vertebrae begin to crack and pop, from the base of my skull down. Something was going to happen. My arm was raising itself...

—

I started throwing up water.

I was on the side of the pool. Someone had pulled me out. Apparently, while I was under the water, my body started convulsing and somebody realized something was wrong. I was told my lips were blue.

I was rushed to the hospital. The doctors said I didn't have any brain damage. I was lucky in that respect. My lungs were damaged from the incident and I ended up with pneumonia, but I survived.

Sometimes I dream about the experience and I remember those moments I touched the hand of the mass. I know I touched it, and I realize that meant something. Because sometimes, if I stare for a long time into a body of water, I can see the black cloud waiting for me.

Sometimes I see it in the mirror.

In My Father's House

I just want to say that this happened to my old man, and he's not the type of guy to have an imagination. He's also not the type to lie. My father grew up in rural New Jersey and went to college in Middle-of-Nowhere, Maine. The college was so small that the classrooms were set up in old, converted chicken coops and they smelled how you'd expect them to. This was years before he enlisted into the Air Force and met my mother. These were his afro days. The 1970s.

My old man had two other roommates that I know of, and they haven't really kept in contact, but they were close at the time. They had found the cabin for cheap. It wasn't advertised—they learned about the availability by word of mouth. Friend of a friend. It had a few rooms and was in decent shape. A few BB holes here and there, mostly in the laundry room. There were some paint spots that needed to be touched up. Brand new shag carpeting. Really, it was a solid find.

The cabin sat on top of a hill with a bit of a yard surrounding it where all the trees were cut down in order to build the place. The driveway was over a mile of rolling hills. The front door opened into a modest living room with a couple of couches and a television with rabbit ears. There were a hallway and a couple of bedrooms, as well as a room for the laundry. It was enough. They had a carport instead of a garage.

My old man and his roommates had lived there for months

without any reason to worry about their circumstances. They'd go to class, come back and pass the time with the sort of antics that young people in Maine do: polar bear dips in the lakes during winter, drunk driving races back when the roads were empty and the drinking laws were pretty lax up, and binge drinking while watching football.

That first winter was going alright. My old man and his buddies made the best of the cold by storing six packs of beer on their living room windowsill to chill before drinking and zoning out to some solid 1970s television. And life was good, until they started to realize that bottles of beer were going missing. A college travesty.

Of the group of them, my father was the big guy. He had lifted weights in high school and worked odd jobs on the farms of northeastern New Jersey, so he was the go-to defender of the group when it came to bar fights and brawls.

One night during a snowstorm he and his roommates realized that another bottle had gone missing.

They decided to act immediately by getting my father layered up and giving him their home protection device: a baseball bat.

Prepared for a confrontation, they hyped up my old man and sent him out into the storm to flank the intruder from the rear of the house. He had a flashlight and was strong enough to run through the snow. But when my father reached the windowsill, there was no sign of anything. No footprints, no empty bottles, no intruder.

They were a bit drunk and it was snowing out, so the group of them decided that even if someone was out there, it was snowing too much to track them down. By the end of the night, the guys figured that it had never happened.

Until it happened again. And a third time.

At one point they argued with each other. It was only after they held a bit of a stakeout and baited the beer-stealer that they confirmed it was not one of the roommates.

Sometimes the bottles disappeared in the evening, other times in the middle of the night while they hung out. They'd go to get a beer only to find themselves a couple short.

Each time after that, my father would be prepped and be sent out to confront the trespasser. And each time he returned with a negative sighting.

After a few weeks of this, they started noticing other little things. Doors would be closed that no one remembered closing. Sometimes the cabin would drop down in temperature, despite the heat being turned all the way up.

Socks started to disappear. This didn't seem too odd; they were a group of college kids, and I said as much to my father when he first told me the story. His response to me was to say that's what he and his roommates thought back then.

But after all the missing beer, they were done explaining things away.

They disassembled the washing machine. It was empty.

They searched every room.

They tightened up the door hinges.

They drew straws and sent out the smallest guy to dig up the snow under the windowsill, in hopes that they would reveal a stack of frozen beers that had somehow slipped off the ledge.

Nothing.

They sent my old man up into the crawl space with the baseball bat and a flashlight. Even the crawl space was empty. No animals, no beers, no socks.

It was in that final moment that the group of young men looked at each other and began to realize something was wrong. Somehow these series of events were connected, and it made them feel uneasy. Their privacy was slowly being invaded and they seemed to be entirely helpless in the midst of the situation.

They decided to research the history of the house and then take whatever they found to the landlord. They started in the public library but there was no way to narrow their search. So they asked a few of the bartenders at the bars they frequented.

The bartenders told the group a story about a miser of a man and his ex-wife, and how the man settled into a low depression and almost drank himself to death. The end of the story involved the man committing suicide with a shotgun in the cabin that my old man and the roommates were living in.

That's why there were BB holes in the walls, the bartender claimed.

My father and his friends were a bit shaken up from the story.

The group discussed all of the events. It was all way more than they expected to hear. They decided to go home and forget the search they were on.

It wasn't late, but the sun was down. For once, it wasn't snowing.

My father was the first one to the front door. Nothing seemed off —all normal.

When my father unlocked and opened the front door, a strange man was standing in front of him. He was an older man with dilated eyes. The stranger wore flannel and was breathing like a smoker having just finished a run in the snow. He wore the type of look you see in the eyes of an animal ready to kill to survive.

Determined hatred.

This intruder was mulling something over to himself, mouthing and tonguing words that weren't really coming out, and moving his lips faster than any of the group was used to seeing. The stranger took the time to make eye contact with everyone there.

There was a brief awkward moment where no one understood what was happening. Then, one of my father's roommates put two and two together: "Are you the dick that's been stealing our beer?"

My father realized this was the moment that he had been drunkenly prepared for countless times. He sobered up a bit from the adrenaline and looked down to see the house's baseball bat sitting there next to the door. As soon as my father picked it up, he squared up to the stranger.

The stranger stood there with a bit of a slouch and a dirty beard. He slacked his jaw and opened his mouth like a snake. There was a popping sound that came from his jaw, as if it was unhinged entirely. The scream that came out was barely that of a man, and it froze my father.

My old man has since confessed that he almost pissed himself in that moment. The stranger's scream was so deeply disturbing to the group that none of them knew how to react. There was only one entrance to the entire house. That doorway my father stood in was the only way out.

Suddenly, a push from one of the roommates behind my father made him cautiously run toward the stranger. The stranger twitched and moved at an amazing speed down the hallway toward the laundry room.

The stranger was able to slam the door behind himself, but my father and the roommates burst through just a second or two after the stranger had closed himself in.

There was no one there.

No footprints outside in the snow in the clear moonlight, no windows or doors open or unlocked. No stranger hiding in the crawl space.

Nothing.

But sometimes their beer would still go missing. And sometimes they'd hear that scream.

This is all based on my father's college life that he experienced in Maine. He was a Jersey boy and the college he attended really was up in Maine in old converted chicken coops. He also really lived in the cabin I described. I'll leave the rest of the story to your imagination.

Glass Houses

Paul used to hear all the jokes from his friends about his living conditions. People rarely made original ones about his place. Sure, the insulation wasn't the greatest, but it was a small one-bedroom and the heating bill could have been worse. Past the house was nothing but a forest bordering the tundra. A desert without sand.

Alaska.

There, the Old West still exists: a final American frontier, where a man is valued by his ability to pull himself up by his bootstraps. A man is a man, a woman a woman, and the universal values of mankind are upheld. Everyone pulls their weight in a place like that. A man trusts his neighbor and the reward is a land of freedom. Territories are still unclaimed, land is still untouched, and the edge of the world is only a nightfall away. Alaska is a younger America, a purer America.

Paul's place had four wall-sized glass doors, one on each side of the building. And when the sun rose, the house was beautiful in the way it sat by itself. At the right angle, it was the only piece of civilization that could be seen on the horizon. Paul's place even had a skylight above his bed. It was a gorgeous lifestyle. Paul and Luke would sit there with a mug of coffee and soak it in. The good life. After losing the wife and kids, Luke was all Paul had. They both needed the free time. They'd go on walks every day, and they'd spend most of their days inside.

Luke would bark at a moose for hours if given the chance, and Paul'd try to stop him, but Luke was a persistent dog. If he ever saw a wolf, it was over: He would be impossible to shut up. Luke was part wolf, part husky, and he could hold his own. He had great instincts, but Paul knew to keep Luke inside if a wolf was ever around. The wolves up there weren't small creatures. If they stood on their hind legs, they'd easily be taller than Paul, and they could weigh around 150 pounds. Luke was a big dog, but he was only 100 pounds and he was solo.

Wolves up there were so big that when Yellowstone was looking to boost its wolf population, the powers that be thought to bring down the Alaskan variety, also known as the Northern Slope Wolf. Entire populations of smaller creatures were almost wiped out. The powers that be had to get rid of the wolves just to save the park.

Sometimes the packs in Alaska would journey through town and attack the local dogs. It got so bad on the Alaskan military posts that they had to open up the laws against killing wolves. They even let the soldiers roll around with live rounds in their personal firearms, which had previously been very illegal. Paul had been in the military for a while. That's why he had first moved to Alaska. He fell in love with the place and when the accident happened, he couldn't leave.

Paul would absorb the culture, the stories of the people of the largest state in America. He once talked to an Eskimo hunting party, which were still allowed to kill and haul whales onto land. They would talk so lackadaisically about how they would have an average of 30 hours before the polar bears would show up to feast on the whale. Paul had never met a group of people so blasé about things that could easily kill them, but who also had their heads screwed on completely right. Alaskans were like that in general. The last pioneers of America. Brave, a little reckless—but he loved them. This was his home. Him and Luke. Luke was a good dog. Loyal. He would protect

Paul to the end of everything. That's why he would bark at everything. Protection.

If one word could ever describe Alaska, that one word would be *quiet*. You could walk for miles and never hear an animal. Sometimes the wind would sit still long enough for a traveler to realize just how alone they were in the expanse.

The "town" Paul lived in was really just a wide swathe of land with a few homes, a gravel road, and a gas station that doubled as a general store. The kind of place where folks could leave their keys in the car. Everyone knew each other's names and the local bar was a good bit of warmth that allowed pets. Luke and Paul would down a few beers and watch the tube while reminiscing about the good days with the old timers. They both spent a few nights there every week or so. The salmon run and the elk herd movements counted as excitement in those parts.

Paul had recently felt himself ache more than usual. It had been a few years since he came home to see what had happened to his family. When he had first gotten Luke, his intent was to have a dog around that could help protect the family. Paul always felt guilty for taking Luke with him into the brush that day. The entire day Luke twitched his ears left and right—he had known something was wrong. All that blood. The red was not often far from Paul's thoughts. It took a few beers a night to be able to think about something else. Paul sometimes felt Luke also was affected by the loss, as he had refused to leave Paul's side.

Last night, Paul was at the kitchen nook when Luke started to act abnormally. More so than usual, so Paul figured it was probably a bear. The town didn't see the big ones often, usually just the garbage eaters. And Luke did a good job of keeping them from tapping on the windows. It was always impossible to tear Luke away from a job like that, and Paul'd long since given up. Luke would get tired when the bear was gone. Maybe it was a wolf.

Paul went to bed.

After a while Luke stopped barking and entered the bedroom. Luke jumped up on the bed and Paul's eyes were adjusted enough to the light to see Luke's hair still on edge. Paul tried to soothe Luke a bit, but Luke nipped at Paul. Luke was still in attack mode. And he had the look in his eyes that said, "Don't get in my way when this goes down." Paul looked to the sliding glass door in the bedroom to see what Luke was concentrating on.

There was a man standing outside the house, on the porch of the glass door. It was October in the tundra, and so it was easily below freezing. But the man standing on the porch wasn't wearing any clothes. Alaskans did some odd things, and this wasn't exactly the craziest thing that Paul had seen… but it was out of character for the townspeople he knew.

The nude man was entirely bald across his whole body, and he was pressing himself up against the glass. The man seemed to have a sort of mud stain all over his frontside. Even with the skylight above the bed, the night wasn't bright enough to illuminate everything, but Paul knew it wasn't mud. Paul couldn't take his eyes off of what he was looking at to get his gun or turn the light on. Breaths were shallow. The mud was dripping from the man's mouth and whatever the mud was, it had stained what few teeth remained in the man's mouth. It didn't take Paul very long to realize that the man wasn't human. Luke knew it, too.

The man proceeded to rub his hands over his frontside between his chest and the glass and then smear the window with the mud. It wasn't a twitchy set of movements, but it was by no means smooth. The entire time, the man maintained eye contact. Even without seeing the eyes, Paul knew they were looking at each other.

There would be more stains the next day when all the bodies

were found in the town.

The man finished smearing the mud and then started to tap on the glass. Luke was ready, his hair was up, but he was unable to bark. Paul's mind was on his family. *So this is how it happened. He's come back.*

Paul saw the man start to reach for the door handle. Alaskans are fiercely independent and revere one another's privacy; this man clearly didn't. Mortals don't make a habit of trekking through the woods in October nights up there. Paul had grown accustomed to living in Alaska, and to living in the type of gas station town where no one locked their sliding glass doors.

I have some friends who were stationed in Alaska and they always tell the greatest stories about living out on the frontier. Some of those bits of information are in this story.

White Heads

Message Board Posting - Not sure what to do... 02:31 AM

I have a few friends who complain about acne all the time, but they never have it as bad as I do. My family is a regular type of middle class family that doesn't really want for anything, but when it comes to my parents being able to afford the meds and pills and stuff to get my skin treated, yeah... that just isn't going to happen. And after tonight, I'm not sure what I'm going to do. I'm kind of freaking out, actually.

The worst thing about having acne as bad as I have it is that no one ever talks about it. They just look at you that certain way. That way where you know exactly what they are looking at. You aren't a person to them, you are a single cluster of zits on a cheek. A freak at the circus.

Dermatologists cost a ton of money, and it's not like we have insurance that'll just pay for it. I've tried all the scrubs and the pads and the ointments from those drug stores. They don't work. I have it real bad. I beg and I beg and my parents cave and buy another thing for twenty bucks off of TV, or from the supercenter. Then I use up the whole tube and nothing really changes. It affects every aspect of my life. Every time I go to the bathroom I have to consider whether or not I should wash my face. Or if I should pop this or squeeze that. If there's blood, I face a choice between being late for or bloody in my next class.

And it's not like I just have acne on my face. I have it everywhere. Like, *everywhere*, everywhere. Well, not my legs, so that's alright. But it's just horrible. My face is where it's the worst. I think I'd give just about anything to clear up my face.

Alcohol pads, brand name stuff, vitamin E, pre- and post-shower scrubs, LED lights, vibrating brushes… I've even tried the whole "wash your pillow every day" plan. It's all a bunch of bullshit if you have real acne. And it sucks. I'm not exactly in shape, so it's not like I'm attractive in other ways that matter to kids my age. It's embarrassing. My friends complain about getting a couple zits and all I can think about is how I'm totally defined by my face.

Everyone I talk to looks at my cheeks, red and pillowy from all of the scar tissue. Sometimes I can feel the scars. But there's nothing I can do. I've made a habit of not squeezing any of them unless they get white. But sometimes that's hard, too. Sometimes I consider using makeup or something. At least girls can just apply a bunch of makeup on and pretend like their faces look normal.

Tonight felt so different, though. Like I said, I can usually feel the scars. Feel the blood in there, and the pus. Sometimes it makes my skin crawl and I can't stand it. Tonight though it was real bad. The current scrub I'm using was something I bought online. It was one of those real New Age websites. The site looked like it was designed through a dude from the 90s using HTML.

It came in a week ago and it's a twice-a-day scrub. It's been making my skin really dry, but it says I'm not supposed to use lotion. So, tonight I was in front of the mirror. And it's the weekend, so I figured I should squeeze anything now so it would get an extra day to heal up before school. There was a really big, white one on my cheek. That one had to go. It had been weird all day, itchy and irritated. This particular one stood out and it felt like my skin was crawling from the inside.

Squeezing properly is, in many ways, an art form. Most of my scars are from when I sucked at squeezing. And I did it too rough and I'd cut myself all up and it'd scab over and everything. I don't scab over these days. I'm a lot smoother throughout the entire process.

While squeezing, I started to feel that lightheaded tingle under my skin. The goosebumps flowed over my body and that feeling, that chalkboard feeling that you're just a little lighter and whiter, ran from my stomach and legs all the way up to inside of me. It's uncomfortable, but it's how I know something's going to finally pop when I'm squeezing.

Of course it hurts. But the cleansing feeling at least feels good when it's all over. But tonight I got really tingly, like something was itching and crawling through my skin and the tingle was everywhere. Right when the tingling feeling was in my arms is when it finally popped.

I felt my skin open and empty as it released whatever is always released from inside of me when I feel that relief. Except, it wasn't really white. And whatever it was was covered in my sticky reddish goop. Then it started crawling over my fingers.

Some sort of insect had grown inside of my face and was still alive.

I totally freaked. There was a larger hole in my face than what I'm used to. And it was housing some sort of bug. I ran from my room to the bathroom and threw the creature into the toilet to flush it down, and then I used all sorts of creams on my face to wash everything clean.

But, while I was looking into the mirror, trying to figure out what the hell had happened, I saw my face again.

It was the first time anything had looked like it was kind of working. Even right now, there's a mirror next to my computer, and all I can do is look at the hole in my cheek. Looking at it makes me feel tingly, but all of the skin around the hole is clean. Not red at all. The real sick part of all of this is that I think I'm going to keep using the lotion, even though I can still feel the itching under my skin and even though I now know what's making me itch.

—

Message Board Post - Not sure what to do… [Update] 12:53 AM

It's been two weeks.

The tube of acne medication is out, but it worked. I think. I'm not sure if I'm actually excited about that or not, because the holes in my face are everywhere now. They're almost worse than the acne was.

Each one is the size of an eraser head, and they're all over my entire body. Not just my face and my chest, or my back. They're everywhere.

I wrote in the comments of the first post that I had woken up that next morning with a few holes in my face. Some of the bugs had broken out of the skin of my face without me squeezing them out. I was a little worried that morning, but I still went to school.

The first day of school after I started using the cream went alright. I expected to get flak from the other kids, but at this point everyone just expects my face to look like it is burned, so no one said anything about the large holes in my face. There were only a few at that point. Probably five.

It was that next night that everything got weird.

I went to bed early because I was feeling a little off. Drained. And I was really itchy, as if my skin was crawling. I applied the acne medication all over. I got into bed in a pair of boxers. Normal.

I woke up in the middle of the night with a dry mouth and

chapped lips. Everything felt sticky, and it was a struggle to move under the blankets. My sheets were covered in sweat. I figured I was sick, and that was why I had felt drained earlier in the night. Probably why I felt like I had goosebumps all over as well. I moved my arm around and rolled over to find my chapstick on the dresser. It was as if I was in some sort of cocoon. I couldn't find the chapstick in the dark, so I turned on the light.

It took a few seconds for my eyes to adjust. I found the chapstick and applied it. I wanted to get up to get a glass of water.

The sheets stuck to me. Once I finally got them off, I realized I wasn't covered in sweat; I was covered in pus. And there were hundreds of bugs. Hundreds, crawling around and squirming in the layer of pus, all over my skin, in my boxers. I coughed out a scream and jumped out of bed. I was covered, and so was my bed. The sheets were supposed to be white, but were instead a black sea of swarming insects, rolling in a frenzy, covered in the pus that had come out of me. Without a second thought, I rolled up all of my sheets and threw them in the washing machine next to the bathroom. Then I ran into the bathroom and jumped into the shower.

I stayed in there for a long time, until I convinced myself that all of the bugs were gone. That every single one had gone down the drain. My body felt empty, like I had a new layer of skin that I had been hiding all along. Except it didn't look new. Every square inch of my body had a hole in it. I stared in the mirror for a long time and couldn't decide if I should scream or cry.

I drank probably a gallon of water, and then went to bed.

Tuesday morning came, and I made my way to the bathroom to see the damage in the sunlight. The initial five holes that those first few bugs had escaped from were turning a deep red. They looked a little swollen, so I squeezed them a little to see if they had anything left in there. A thick black ooze began to seep from the holes. I looked at the rest of the holes that had since covered my body, and knew the black pus would be covering my bed a night later.

I've since been in my room. The school told my parents I went home sick. It's been a week since I first started the tube of medication. None of the bugs are left, but the holes are everywhere.

I've been looking at them, though, and the black pus eventually has stopped. Not only that, the original five holes are healing, and it doesn't look like they're going to scar up. My skin looks more clear than it has ever been.

I'm afraid of what the kids at school are going to say when I go back on Monday. My acne was so bad, I doubt the single tube was enough. As messed up as this all has been, I ordered another.

—

Message Board Post - Not sure what to do… [Final Update] 06:39 PM

This has all completely spiraled out of, it's all…

Where do I even begin with something like this? I just wanted to get rid of my face. All the scars and the acne and the torment that went along with it.

I used the the entire tube of acne medication that I got, and, well, you know what happened. I ended up taking a week off from school after all the holes got really bad and all the bugs finally crawled out. Even thinking about it makes my skin turn into a giant desert of rolling goosebumps.

Initially, when I realized it was working, I ordered more. Which in hindsight was an act of desperation, but I just wanted it to be gone. I waited long enough, but the next tube never showed up. When I tried calling the customer support service, I was transferred to some foreign company's answering machine.

All of my evidence and possible evidence was gone. The insects had all died and I burned the sheet they had been wrapped in before even thinking of the possible ramifications. I dumped the bugs in the sand in the corner of my backyard, since they were just exoskeletons at that point. Figured the local animals would eat them and the birds would get a bit of a feast. My mother has always been the type to throw our leftovers out on the back porch and let the stray cats eat anything that we can't eat. Sometimes she even takes the strays to the vet if she thinks they're sick. I figured leaving the bugs out there would be about the same type of charity.

We have an old dog named Max in the backyard, too, but he doesn't do too much these days. He spends almost all of his time sticking halfway out his dog house. There once was a time when he wouldn't even let a bird land in the yard. But now, if a cat sat on his nose Max would probably just lay there. Max is so old that he doesn't even get up when we feed the cats scraps. He just watches and waits for us to fill up his dog bowl.

If I knew it would get this bad, I wouldn't have done that. I would have tried to do something about the insects. It's not like I haven't. The company's website completely disappeared. Their phones were all apparently disconnected. It was like none of it ever existed.

The shower that I had washed so many of the bugs down into had one of those drains with some pretty sizable holes. I had assumed that once I washed the bugs down, that would be it. They'd go down and live out their tiny lives. But they didn't. Somehow they were able to stay in the drain. After a few days, I took a shower and I saw some of them sticking their long legs through the grate of the shower drain. They weren't that tiny anymore. They reached out with their legs like they wanted to get back to me, like they wanted to touch my skin again.

I ran to the store to use the last of my allowance money on as much off-label drain unclogger as I could find. I dumped gallons down that drain until they were all gone. Still, the survival of the shower group made me want to check on the pile in the backyard.

None of them were there anymore. None. Not only that, I saw trails and markings from where they had crawled away. They had all lived, and they were out there.

A few days after the revelation that the bugs were still alive and had grown, I noticed a lack of neighborhood cats running around. There was usually an orange tomcat that had claimed our backyard as its home, but even he was missing. Max seemed fine, though, so I wasn't exactly sure what was going on.

I finally saw the tomcat in our backyard a couple days after I noticed all the animals missing. I quickly went outside to see how he was doing. He seemed to be scratching a lot and I wanted to see if he had fleas or not so I could get one of the spare flea collars from the garage. When I got closer to him, though, I saw that he was scratching patches in his fur. He let me touch him and I moved his fur around and saw that the tomcat had the same holes in his skin that I had from the acne medication.

It wouldn't have been much of a problem if it was the same type of thing as I had gone through. But it wasn't. The holes I had in my face were nothing compared to the size of the holes in the poor tomcat's skin. Not only were the insects out there, but they were apparently growing. And they were leaving bigger holes.

Kids started to not show up to school. Each day more and more kids were absent, and it started to get around that something was happening. There was talk that some kids had to have plastic surgery, the holes in their skin were so large.

I tried telling my parents and even the police, but the story was so out there that no one believed me. And I didn't have any proof.

Everyone was too busy trying to figure out how to handle the issue at hand.

Today was the worst of all. Today, while I was walking home from school, I saw what must have been some of the original insects. It was a roving pack of them. Hundreds. Each of them the size of a kitten, with wiry legs full of fur. The insects had the heads of some type of rhinoceros beetle and shiny black shells. They crossed the street in front of me and I saw them scurry over the fence that led to my backyard. And then I heard the most terrible high pitched screaming I have ever heard. By the time I got to Max, there wasn't much of him left. It was pretty quick, maybe a couple minutes. But he screamed the entire time. He didn't deserve that.

I figure it's a little too late to say sorry. I don't know who to tell. What to do next.

What to do. All I wanted was to be normal.

I had acne really bad during the end of high school and into my time at the Academy. It only got worse when I was in college and never saw the sun. It probably didn't help that it was a stressful environment. I hated every minute I had acne, and it made me pretty image-conscious. The idea of bugs being in a cream was really just a vehicle for me to write about how crappy it was to have terrible acne as a young man. My lovely wife was able to see past that, and these days I have a mostly non-monster-like appearance.

Orpheus's Lot

Back in middle and high school there were rumors that there existed a game that was capable of summoning demons. Why middle schoolers were so obsessed with the idea of calling forth such things remains understood only to middle schoolers.

I would hear weird stuff like that all the time, though. My family lived in a small town out in Wyoming and the remoteness of the place brought on all sorts of odd stories. I never put much stock in them. I didn't believe in demons, or any fantasies, really. I saw little point in games with doubtful outcomes, so my knowledge of the game was entirely second-hand.

The kids would always talk about how they were going to try the game and see what happened, but no one ever seemed to actually finish it. The rules progressively got more intense; self-mutilation eventually became a factor. Again, from my perspective, this was all foolish. Why pluck an eye or rip some hair to presumably summon a devil? But middle schoolers have many kinds of logic.

Obviously, some kids tried it. Some did it driven by the hormones of adolescence; others, I'm sure, did it for social currency. Perhaps one or two did it for genuine scientific curiosity. In all cases, none ever completed the rite.

The game was called Orpheus's Lot. I know that sounds pretty deep for a kid's game, and we never knew where the name came from.

We all learned of the game around seventh grade. By the time I made it to high school we started to hear rumors about kids actually completing it. None of us thought it was true, but the notion of someone finishing the game was nevertheless intriguing.

There was one boy named Danny who used to say he knew a lot about the game. That he had done it, and that he had come close to finishing it by himself.

The will required to finish the game by oneself was incomprehensible to most of us, based on our knowledge. The game was so odd and so gruesome in parts that you had to have a partner who could assist you.

But Danny said he almost finished. That the last time he tried it he got to the last step when he passed out.

Danny was not the type of kid we would have considered cool. Not that I was one of the cool kids, but Danny was one of the lowest on the scale of popularity. Looking back on it, I don't believe Danny had any friends. My one friend Andrew would sit with him at lunch from time to time, but that was more out of pity than enjoyment, I think. Andrew was a good guy, and he likely thought Danny could use the kindness. Not only that, Andrew's parents were best friends with Danny's parents.

If I'm to be completely honest, it would have been hard to be Danny's friend even if we were inclined to be. It was as if he wanted everyone to think he was a weird kid. He'd act out in class and recite facts about wars and guns needlessly. He wasn't really in shape, but he talked almost exclusively about the military. He was pretty off. And for the most part, we simply let him do his thing.

There was one kid, though, who really despised Danny. It was almost like the two were storybook nemeses. The other kid's name was Erikson. He had a first name, though no one called him by it. Erikson was pretty popular, and he was the type of kid who would go out of his way to make someone feel like a lesser human being. When Danny joined the soccer team, Erikson quit baseball and joined soccer, just to show Danny up. Any time Danny tried to start a club, Erikson would join it just to poke fun at him.

Erikson was a pretty despicable kid. Everyone knew it, even back then. But for some reason, everyone also wanted him to like them. He had transcended the popularity contest to become what was popular. Everything he did was the cool thing to do.

Erikson had heard Danny bragging around that he had almost finished the game by himself. And just to call poor Danny out, Erikson exclaimed that he would finish the game by himself that night.

This was truly unprecedented. The entire point of summoning the demon was for it to—allegedly, mind you—whisper secrets from "the other side" to you. Apart from aiding in one finishing the summoning rite, one's partner was also ostensibly to prevent the demon from attaching itself to one's body in exchange for knowledge.

Danny didn't have any friends, so he had to do it alone. It was his only option. Looking back, I could see his motivations: not just to meet the demon, but to also be the kid who completed the game. And to have been the kid who did it by himself. The kid was able to do all of those things to himself unaided, and still have the strength to keep the alleged demon at bay.

Erikson didn't show up to school the next day. Nor did Danny.

And a few days passed, and Danny eventually came to school with stitches and a huge scar on his face. We couldn't see the whole scar, because he was wearing an eye patch. He was also missing a couple of his fingers.

The rumor was that he had ripped his own eye out.

The look Danny had on his face made me believe it. He didn't say a word. He was a different kid. No one tried to ask him if he finished the game—whether he had or not, none of us questioned his commitment.

A few weeks after that, I was hanging out with Andrew. Andrew said Danny had talked to him about what had happened.

Apparently, Danny was performing the steps of the game. He did the salt and the candles, the drawings with the chalk, the urine, and the drinking: Danny said he performed all the steps for the three hours we thought they were supposed to be performed in. And then he started the last part, the cuttings.

The last part was tricky, because every kid who knew a lot about the game seemed to make up his own stuff once the cutting step was initiated. Danny believed that the face was crucial, and he was prepared to go all the way. Danny said he cut into the skin on his face, and the moment the first drop of blood touched the pentagram Danny lost all control of his body. He said he was still kneeling there, but he wasn't controlling his hand. He didn't have any power over the knife and it slid all the way down his forehead. When he got to his eye he said he tried to resist, but he had no control. The knife slid down and cut through his closed eyelid and into his eye socket. He used the knife to work the eye and his other hand yanked it out and squeezed the juice into the center of the pentagram on the floor.

Danny described it as the most painful thing he had ever experienced. The pain did more than make his head spin—it altered his perception of color, distance, and shapes. One moment he was kneeling on the pentagram and the next he was a leg of the pentagram, and then moments or hours later there seemed to be no pentagram. The only constant was the blood, and the lapping sound it made as it flowed freely and endlessly.

That's when the demon's fingers breached the filmily layer of blood on the floor.

First the hand.

Then the arm appeared.

Then the head and the torso.

The demon pulled itself out of the ground, where the blood had pooled the most. It was a slow process. Once it was through the portal, the ground solidified and the demon leaned back on its hoofs in a crouch. It had golden eyes that burned as it stretched its neck and jaws. The hoofs, neck, jaws, eyes: these were all Danny remembered. And the blood. And his inability to do anything except kneel in a petrified stupor.

The demon moved forward and put its hands over Danny's stomach. It blinked and Danny's shirt disappeared. It was looking Danny in the eye when suddenly it looked down and turned its gaze to the floor.

It jumped back through the blood portal and Danny said it was as if nothing had ever happened. That his shirt was back on. He ran to his parents, crying, and they took him to the emergency room. He rested a few days, and then came back to school.

Andrew said Danny told the story as if it were all real, but we were all inclined not to trust Danny's word. He did, after all, have that annoying habit of spouting off encyclopedia facts on obscure topics for no reason except to elicit the occasional "atta-boy" from someone.

Danny was never really the same at school. He was a lot more quiet. He even made a few more friends due to his calmer nature. Andrew would talk with me about it every once in a while. He said Danny would sometimes call him extremely late at night and rave endlessly about crucifixes, voodoo, and the occult. Danny was pretty sure he was damned for getting as far in the game as he did.

Then the police report came out about Erikson. The entire town talked about it. Everyone knew. Danny went missing for another day and the rumor after that was that the police had come in and were questioning everyone involved. Erkison's parents were suspected, but the evidence indicated, pretty clearly, that Erikson had done all of the things to himself.

And his body… Erikson had gone home the same night as Danny had, and had done all of the rituals. He poured the wax on himself, he sliced open his lip, he broke one of his toes. When Erkison's parents found his body, he was laying on the floor of his bedroom, on top of the pentagram drawn in chalk. He had sliced himself up with a knife from their kitchen.

He was holding his eyes in his hands. An eye per hand. His stomach had been sliced wide open, and the hole in his gut was in the shape of a pentagon.

His parents were pretty quiet about it. No one in the town ever saw them after that, and none of us blamed them for anything. The police didn't convict them of anything. Andrew said his parents went over to the Eriksons' house to try and console them. The only thing the Eriksons ever said about it all was that Erikson never screamed. There were no sounds of warning. They simply found him there on the floor the next morning, with his intestines pulled out and covering the floor.

A few years after that, Danny killed himself in much the same way.

In addition to the proliferation of short horror stories online, there's also been a growth in "horror games," mostly among middle school-aged kids. Sometimes kids will do the the game and then go onto message boards and tell everyone how they completed the ordeal.

I wanted to write something no one would want to actually do, and I wanted to write what would happen if a kid did it. I was careful to not include the steps, and I made a lot of it ambiguous for the same reason. I didn't want some kids cutting themselves up and then some random parent saying that their kid read my story and was convinced to do these or those actions.

The real intent was to have a discussion about why kids do things like that. Is it for attention, or curiosity, or popularity, or conformity?

I'm no different. I was a middle school boy once, and I experienced the pressures of masculinity in our society. To say that I didn't give in to peer pressure would be a lie. Of course I did. These days, I'm in the Army and my record is full of schools and my chest has well-over the required sixteen pieces of flair. Napoleon was right when he said that a soldier will fight long and hard for a bit of colored ribbon.

American men challenge ourselves to achieve ultimately pointless achievements in pursuit of our sense of masculinity. A lot of American masculinity is based on the pointless episodes of masochism: Tough Mudders, marathons, fist fights, Ranger School. We want to prove ourselves so we can then brag to our friends that we found out so much about our limits.

Cold Static

I died again last night—it was uncomfortable and full of static. I'm not really sure how old I am anymore, but I think I'm in my early twenties.

Sometimes it's quiet, sometimes it isn't. The morning after it happens, I just, like—I wake up, alive and unharmed. Like some twisted *Groundhog Day*. The difference is that I'll be an entirely different person.

Sometimes I'm older, sometimes I'm younger. I was originally born a girl, I think. But after so many bodies, I'm not really sure anymore. I think rather asexually these days.

The first time it happened I had a hard time dealing with the change. I had never been in a car accident before.

I saw the other car coming, but there was so much snow, I didn't know what to do. I was only sixteen, and it shouldn't have happened. I mean, I was a late bloomer—I had just figured out all that period crap, had my first boyfriend. I laugh when I think of how young I was.

And then the other car hit. It happened quickly, but not so quickly that I don't remember the pain. It was an older car. Mine was, that is. My parents wanted my first car to be a beater. The steering wheel did something. My breasts were completely crushed into my ribcage. I felt my bowels let go. I almost died from bleeding out, but both lungs had collapsed.

I sat there in total shock and total pain. At first I was angry. Then I tried to pray but the thoughts were too random. I'm not sure how long this all went about, but by the end I just wanted it to go black, and mercifully it did. The pain was everywhere. Choking on your own blood induces a claustrophobic response. I didn't realize until many deaths later what had happened. Now I'm familiar with the sensation, but that first time... I was so afraid. I just wanted out of the car, out of my broken body. I wanted the men and women driving by to just stop looking at me and actually help me.

I try to keep reminding myself of that death because I want it to be the first one. It's vivid, and clear, but sometimes I remember things differently. Sometimes it feels like I was born a boy and my first death was a drowning. Sometimes I feel like I died of old age in Canada twenty years ago.

I've since died of broken hips, shootings, strokes, rabies, liver failure, cancer, and suicide. Cancer is not an easy way to leave. And suicide, yeah, I felt a pretty intense moment of regret when I fell.

I've woken up in the bodies of priests, doctors, Taliban fighters, garbage men, CEOs, senators, fast food employees, and single moms. Sometimes it's a really depressing life, sometimes it's amazing, and sometimes it's affluent. I've also learned amazing doesn't always equal affluent, but it usually does. I'm always aware that I'll die in a few days. So, if I can, I do try to enjoy it.

I mean, their death is my life.

Sure, when it started happening I thought it was amazing. After the shock of the first few bodies I felt more comfortable. If I woke up in a married man or woman's body, well, I was a teenager stuck in those bodies. I could see what it was like to have kids, to make love, what it is like to be surrounded by loving strangers on your deathbed. How to take a shower without the use of my legs.

I've been experiencing aspects of humanity that no one ever gets to talk about. Having to use a laxative suppository just to go to the bathroom… yeah. That took me a few days to figure out. Since then, I've had a lot more respect for the wheelchair-bound experience.

I've been beautiful women, I've had beer bellies, I've gone clubbing, been a very awkward stripper, lived in a Samoan's body, and even flown a plane. No, I didn't crash it; we landed safely, thanks to the copilot. I died of a heart attack later that night.

I'll wake up in strange places sometimes. Normally I'll be in a bed, though. I'll wake up before I open my eyes and I'll let the air fill my nostrils. Every part of the world smells different. I've gotten to the point where I can guess where I am.

I've leaned in for kisses, and felt the warmth of making love to a stranger who cried beautifully during the experience. I've hugged my children. I've given high fives to communists. I've watched the great silverbacks. I've died giving birth to beautiful twin boys. And I've looked down from the Alps.

But those are the good lives. I've died as a child, as a prisoner, as a gangbanger, everything.

I've been raped and murdered before. Both as a man and as a woman.

I've been the gas station employee robbed and killed for fifty dollars in a register.

I've been a North Korean boy, alone in a gulag.

I've felt desperation while my intestines fell through my fingers. I've blinked my eyes after being beheaded.

I've been a casualty in several wars. Those aren't easy lives: to just wake up and I'm supposed to be a member of a group of soldiers and to not let them down. Sometimes I'm the only one hit, and my countrymen carry me for miles to try and save me. I've gotten better at last words when I'm able to, but those first few times, looking up into a man's eyes... I just knew I was supposed to be this guy's best friend. He had done so much to save me, and the words I needed to express, well, they were lost inside me. I just froze up, feeling the pain of the experience. Those lives are the most beautiful to experience, but I always feel guilty the next morning when I wake up. I at least get to escape those wars.

I've looked up my previous lives, tried to find the pattern. There isn't one. Sometimes I'm an American, sometimes I'm not. I've woken up on every continent. Antarctica is lonely, but serene. Germans party all night just like the South Koreans. The streets of Saudi Arabia feel like the streets of Mexico City. England is beautiful when it isn't raining. The Great Pyramids are perfect. The world is beautiful.

Now I'm 14, again, this time I'm a woman—a girl. Next time I'll probably be a man.

I'm only saying all of this because I think I've figured it out. I think I'm supposed to give fulfillment to these families before I die, as though I'm supposed to wrap up these lives as best as I can. But this one right now... I'm not sure. As far as I can tell, the body and I are the same, and we share the experience. I feel their emotions as well as my own. So I'm pretty sure they can see everything I'm doing. From reviewing their thoughts, I get the gist of who they were. Most of them hang out a lot online, but who doesn't these days? All I know is that they are all in slumps when I reach them. Some are truly depressed.

We begin life with promises and potential. The American Dream is a human endeavor. We start out, unafraid. We fall while walking, we babble nonsense. That's how we grow and how we learn. Somewhere throughout our lives we grow afraid to just take it all in and live. There's nothing to be afraid of. The beauty of life is in the little imperfections, and in finding the grace to experience that beauty in real time.

I'm not entirely sure what I've become, and what it means. Maybe I'm not anything besides a consciousness. Maybe none of us are. Maybe that's supposed to be the point of all of this.

Letter From The Author

This entire collection could be attributed to me meeting a man named Patrick Albright a little over a year ago. I was stationed at Fort Benning, Georgia, and happened to be working in a Public Affairs Office (PAO). Through a series of circumstances and coincidences, Pat and I worked alongside each other (I'll be more than happy to explain more if you ever ask) and I started to write, again. It had been a few years since I finished any writing; now there's enough for this collection.

I was the only uniformed member of an office filled with civilians. I tried to learn as much as possible from them because I thought that everything they were doing was interesting. The PAO is the office in the military that talks to the media and communicates directly to the civilian populace. When news is released, it goes through them. They make Army videos, and they even have combat cameramen. All that footage we get to see on the *History Channel* is from PAO types.

They also run the Facebook pages for the Army, which is one of the jobs I picked up while I was there because I thought it would be fascinating. And it was. I had 200,000 users that I would interact with. I was able to help a lot of parents and answer a lot of questions. I was interviewed (interrogated) by *USA Today* once, and spoke to a senator's office on another day. It was a great job. I learned a lot about the Army that I hadn't known before sitting in that cubicle.

Along with the job came some really cool co-workers. Ex-military types, military spouses, and regular civilians who were just awesome at their jobs. And my cubicle neighbor was Pat. Pat was really into film, just like me, and we talked about movies basically every day. Pat was one of the photographers, and after a couple months he showed me that he enjoyed making horror movies in his free time, which I thought was really cool. So I showed him a short story I had written with my friend Marcellus.

Pat really liked it and we talked about writing and horror for days. Eventually, I suggested that he and I collaborate on a project together. He agreed immediately. What we first started working on was a short film. That grew into a feature length project which I'm actually going to finish after I am done with this collection.

The biggest hiccup was that I had never written horror before. I was a fan: I loved movies like *The Shining*, *Alien*, *The Thing*, *Frailty*, and I enjoyed reading Edgar Allen Poe, Stephen King and H.P. Lovecraft, but that was all I really had as a frame of reference, so I decided to work on horror by writing short stories. Eventually, I found a Reddit.com sub called /r/NoSleep, and I saw a perfect opportunity to write and post stories online. So I did. Now I've written a collection.

Overall, this has been a very fulfilling creative experience. Five years ago, I couldn't have looked forward into my life and seen myself writing a graduate thesis, let alone a collection of short horror stories.

This collection began with thirty stories. It was whittled down by the test readers and my faithful editor, Tony, to what is now this current collection. I really struggled with the order of the stories, especially which story should be read first and which story should be read last. I tried to order them in such a way that they would flow and not be too overbearing in their similarities. As difficult as selecting the first story was, the final story was the most challenging to select. I feel that by selecting *Cold Static* as the final story, I've let the stories end by allowing them to speak for themselves.

To speak a little more on horror in general, I've always been attracted to it as a genre because it encompasses so many base human emotions. There's a raw honesty to horror, to what a human will do in a fearful situation. Concepts like fight or flight deprive us of our illusions of control. Writing a character in a horror project is interesting to me because I get to think about who that person is in their most raw form. Strip everything away and put a knife in a stranger's hand and ask yourself what would really happen: there's something very intimate about that moment of discovery as a writer.

Unrelated to the genre, I wrote most of this book listening to the same six-ish songs. None of them are related to horror, but maybe you would enjoy listening to them, too: *Outro* by M83, an arrangement of a piano piece from the film *Cloud Atlas* performed by a YouTuber called Mark Fowler, *Four Seasons (Winter)* by Vivaldi, *Fish* by Leningrad (live version), *Madness* by Muse, and *My Body is a Cage* performed by Peter Gabriel. I also listened to Arcade Fire's version of *My Body is a Cage*, so I guess that counts as seven. I suck songs dry by putting them on repeat for hours until I no longer receive inspiration from the music. Then I put them at the bottom of the list, and start up the next song until the same happens. After a while the song will inspire me again. It's always worked for me.

I hope you enjoyed these stories as much as I enjoyed writing them. I have several other projects that I intend to continue working on, and this will definitely not be my last venture into the horror genre. Or the short horror story, for that matter. Again, thank you for reading, ladies and gentlemen.

Ashley Franz Holzmann
Fayetteville, North Carolina
September, 2014

Special Thanks

Ladies and gentlemen,

First off, I would like to thank you for reading this anthology. Without you, I would have to just force my wife to read all of these stories and be the sole evaluator on whether or not I should let them see the light of day. Whether you found me through my Reddit.com posts, under my AsForClass handle, or from another method of social media or book retailing, I think it's pretty wild. So thank you for that.

Second, (but first in my heart) I would like to thank my wife for her eternal support. I have time-consuming hobbies, and I can be obsessive. She is the greatest of sports about it and a truly supportive woman.

Next, my test readers Walter and Sophie, who are my first critics and who gave me invaluable advice when it came to writing what has become this book. Walter and Sophie were more than willing to put in the hours of reading and critiquing based solely on our friendship, and that's a pretty awesome thing.

Tony, my editor, classmate, and former roommate from the Academy—you're amazing. I like that you're reading this right now and trying to decide whether or not you should tell me to cut this sentence out. Or this fragment. That fragment was for you, buddy. Please make my grammar sound good. Who knew we would be working together on projects like this all those years ago?

I would also like to thank my friend, Pat, who got me into the horror genre to begin with.

Finally, I would like to thank my parents for fostering whatever they fostered inside of me that drives me to continue to be a creative person. I don't know how it worked, but something you did sparked within me a desire to constantly create. Whatever that something was, you are to blame. I couldn't have accomplished any of my creative endeavors without you.

Thank you all.

About The Author

Ashley Franz Holzmann was born in Okinawa, Japan and raised in a variety of countries while his parents served in the Air Force. He considered attending art school, but is instead a graduate of West Point, where he enjoyed intramural grappling and studying systems engineering and military history. He majored in sociology and is currently a captain in the Army. Ashley speaks Korean, enjoys backpacking, and is the cook in his family. He currently lives in North Carolina with his wife, two sons, and their two dogs.

Thank you for taking the time to read The Laws of Nature. If you enjoyed the experience, please consider telling your friends or posting a short review. Spreading the word is the greatest way to show support and much appreciated.

If you have enjoyed his artwork or reading his stories, you can talk to Ashley on Facebook at www.facebook.com/AsForClass. For more information, please bookmark www.asforclass.com.

26245462R00104

Made in the USA
San Bernardino, CA
22 November 2015